HERGÉ

THE ADVENTURES OF TINTIN

LAND OF BLACK GOLD

الذَّهَبُ الأَسْوَدُ

EGMONT

This edition first published in 1992
by Methuen Children's Books,
Reprinted in 2003 by Egmont Books Limited,
239 Kensington High Street, London W8 6SA

10 9 8 7 6 5 4

ISBN 0 416 18600 9

Land of Black Gold

Printed in Spain

LAND OF BLACK GOLD

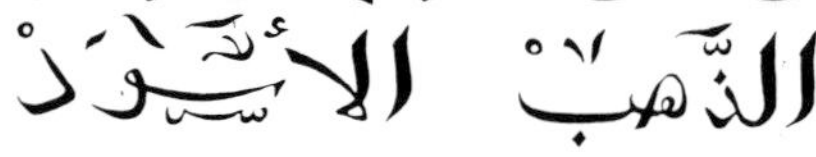
الذَّهبُ الأسْوَدْ

O.K!... O.K! ... I'm coming!
TOOOT
TOOOT
TOOOT
TOOOT
TOOOT

Half a gallon...
Think it'll go in?

And you can save a few drops for my lighter ...

As your lordship pleases ...

TOOOT
TOOOT

Let's have some music ... Radio Luxembourg ...
There! ...
755543

Boom! ... One day your car goes Boom ... Don't just give up in gloom ... Call Autocart to the rescue
755543

Boom! ... One day your car goes Boom!
Boom!

!
!
BOOM

?
?

Now I understand why they call it an internal combustion engine!
This is no time for cheap jokes! We need a breakdown gang ...

Precisely ... But where from ?
Hmmm ... yes..

Saved ! ... Look ! ... There's a tele-phone box.

SEND FOR Autocart
SEND FOR Autocart

Hello ... Autocart to the rescue ! ... Yes ... Yes ... the B0493 ... 8 miles ... Yes ... Mr. Thompson

Well ? ...
A breakdown truck will be here in half an hour.

Let's have a cigarette while we wait ...

Thanks.

CLICK

BOOM

?
?

Next morning ...

"Crisis deepens-official" "On the brink of war?" "Are we prepared?"... "Call-up for army reserve"... "Forces on standby". Things look bright, I must say.

RRRRING
RRRRING

Yes... Tintin here... Oh, hello Captain... How are you?... Any news?

I've just had Admiralty orders: "Captain Haddock. Immediate. Proceed to assume command of merchant vessel blank blank" (the name's secret, of course) "at blank, where you will receive further orders." So that's that ... I've been mobilised! ... No, there won't be time to see you. I'm off right away... I'll keep in touch ... 'Bye, Tintin.

Goodbye, Captain, and good luck. Let's hope it's only a false alarm ...

RRRRING

Hello!
Good morning. What news?

What news! Plenty! Something very odd has just happened!
To be precise ... we just happen to be very odd!
Really? Tell me about it. Come on in...

Well, we'd just filled up with petrol and were driving peacefully along, when all of a sudden, without a word of warning ... our car went ...

BOOM

It seems to be catching!
841201

It certainly is... That's exactly what happened to us!
Yes. And that's not all...

A few minutes later my cigarette lighter, filled at the same pump, blew up in my hands ...
The petrol... it must have been ...

...doctored, yes! ... That's what suddenly occurred to us... And if it was doctored, it must have been done by someone with an interest in wrecked cars. Remember the old police maxim: Who profits from the crime?

Now, who stands to gain from this business? ... Who, eh? ... I'll tell you! ... the breakdown people, Autocart!
!

No doubt about it : Autocart doctors the petrol. When the engine blows up, you send for a breakdown truck. And who do you call? The people who do the most advertising : Autocart!
I suppose it's possible, but...

No buts! It's a certainty!... We're taking up the case, and by this time next week we'll have enough evidence to arrest the entire board of directors.
Good luck to you!...

For a start, we'll take a snoop around the Autocart garage...

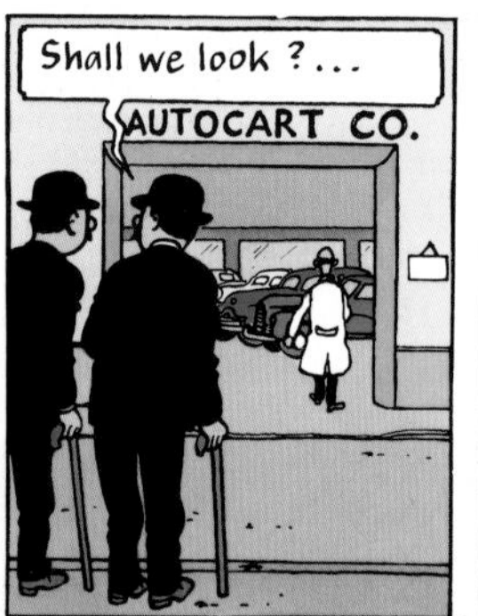
Shall we look ?...
AUTOCART CO.

WANTED
Good drivers with mechanical experience to man breakdown trucks
APPLY Autocart

Well, what do you think ?... It's a perfect cover... gives us a chance to see what goes on inside the place...
Good idea...

Next day...
Now, you know what you're supposed to be doing ?
Certainly we do, sir!
Autocart
53
121572

I must say, I'm intrigued by this petrol business ...
?

I'd like to get to the bottom of it...
You aren't starting another of your adventures are you? Why don't we retire?

SPEEDOL

The managing director, please
ENQU

Meanwhile...
Hello! Autocart to the rescue... Yes... Yes... B 0494 ... For Mr... ?

...Thomson ...It's... the breakdown truck...it's... er... broken down!
SEND FOR Autocart

Would you like to comment, sir, on the situation created by the deterioration in petrol quality ...
Catastrophic! The situation is catastrophic ...

Look! In two months, consumption has dropped by 65 % ... And it's falling every day ... This very morning ...
SALES CHART

... the airline companies decided to suspend all services because of the dangers of fuel explosions in the air ... Oil shares have slumped to half their value ... the bottom's dropping out of the market ... It's a disaster! ... A catastrophe! ...

Even worse! What about the international situation? ... Supposing war comes ... breaks out tomorrow? ... Imagine what'll happen ... Ships ... planes ... tanks ... The armed forces, completely immobilised! ... The mind boggles! ... Disaster!

What do you think has caused this sudden change in the petrol?
That's the question we'd all like to answer! Nothing has changed at the oilfields, or in the refineries, so it has to be sabotage ...

We took samples at the wells, from storage depots, aboard the tankers, in the refineries, and we had them analysed ... Nothing! Absolutely nothing! Then we decided to treat the petrol itself, to prevent it exploding. Our top scientists are working night and day on the problem ... to find some way of ...

BOOM
?
?

Another car blowing up! ... Where was I? Oh yes ... My senior research officer says they are on the verge of success in our labs ... I'm expecting a call from him any moment now to say they've found the solution ...

That'll be him ... Do you mind? ...
No, of course ...
RRRING
RRRING

Yes? ... Well, you've got it? ... An answer? ... What? ... Nothing at all? ... Nothing? ... I see ... Well, it's a pity ... You'll just have to keep at it ...

SALES CH

What? ... Should you go on with the research? Of course ... surely that's obvious ... Why bother to ask? ...

Because if we're to go on, sir, you'll have to consider building a new laboratory!

Analysis of the petrol showed nothing... but what if someone used an additive that leaves no trace?...Tonight, Snowy my friend we'll take a little trip to see some storage tanks...

ELECTRA

GENERAL MOBILISATION

Meanwhile at Autocart...
Ice?!... Ice on the road! What sort of fool d'you take me for?...I'll give you one more chance...but watch your step!... Understand?...Go and check the tyre pressures on the boss's car!
FRIDAY 13 AUGUST

Anyway, we're better off here at the garage. More likely to get inside information...

My car ready, Vic?
In a minute, sir. We're just checking your tyre pressures.
Ssh! It's the manager.

How are things going, Vic? As bad as ever?
Afraid so...

It looks black... Everyone's talking of war... they say things could blow sky high at any moment...

BANG

That night...

Aha! There are the tanks...

?
PHWEEE

Ah! You've come! ...Have you got it?
Yes. Here... Where's the cash?
SPEED

There.
O.K... You leave tomorrow?
Aaah... Aaaaah... Aah...
Yes. 'Speedol Star' sails on the afternoon tide.

TCHOOO

If someone's snooping, he's had his chips!

It's only a dog... Just as well!...

Don't let's hang around: someone might come!... Goodbye!...
Goodbye!... and good luck!

Good old Snowy! That was a near thing... I believe we're on to something... The next move is to ring my contact at Speedol.

Hello?... Yes... Oh, good evening Tintin... A clue? ... You really think so?... Are you sure that's wise? There could be a war any day... What's that? Aboard 'Speedol Star' as radio officer?... All right, I'll lay it on for you.

Next morning ...
SPEEDOL STAR

So you're the new radio officer... You look a bit young to me...
You think so?...

Hello, Thompson?... Oh, it's Thomson... Jebb here, at headquarters... You're to join the 'Speedol Star' as deckhands... sailing today for Khemikhal, the chief port in Khemed... There's a row going on there between the Emir, Ben Kalish Ezab and Sheik Bab El Ehr who's trying to depose him... Khemed is dynamite... Keep your eyes open...

You heard?...
Yes... We've just got time to pack ourselves up...

Tell me, my man, where is our cabin ?

... and the next time you open your big mouths you'll address me as 'captain'... Understand ?

TOOOOT
POOL STAR

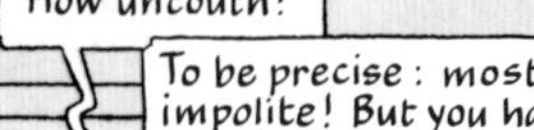
How uncouth!

To be precise : most impolite! But you have to admit, he's got plenty of push ...

Now we must mingle discreetly with the crew...We don't want to attract attention ...

16

What the...?! It's that dog I saw last night!!

Maybe just a co-incidence...Still, can't be too careful...

I need a safer hiding place for the goods...

Hey, you...
Who?... Me?... What?... When?...

Police?
Special Branch, yes... But...er ...how did you know?

It's my job to know everything... Allow me to introduce myself: Jock McPhee of Naval Intelligence, on a top-secret mission...
Thomson and Thompson of Special Branch... also deadly secret...

I'd like you to do something for me... take care of some secret documents... Someone's on to me and may try to steal them ...OK?
Anything for a colleague!

That's fixed that!... Now I can relax...

?

Just wait till we reach Khemikhal... you and your master!

No... I'll fix you right now, my friend!

...massive troop movements are also reported...The Prime Minister told the House today that the world situation is grave, but the government has taken all steps necessary to meet an emergency ...

The news goes from bad to worse... One single spark could set the world ablaze ...

Hello, where's Snowy? ...I've heard enough for today... Snowy!...Snowy! ... Oh, he's gone out...

Golly! Some bone!
?

GRR GRRR
WOOAH

WOOAH WOOAH

Hello?...
Hello?...

Hey, Sparks!... trying to call up Mars?... Here's a message for the company... I want a reply right away...

Aye, aye, Captain!

TAP... TAP TAP
TAP... TAP TAP

War... It's horrible ... I can't get it out of my mind... Surely to goodness the statesmen will come to their senses

BEEP BEEEP BEEP
BEEP BEEP BEEEP
Ah! That'll be the reply from head office...

I'll be back in a minute, Snowy.

Why, it's dark already...

The reply from the company?... Good ... Thanks, Sparky.
Goodnight, Captain.

That's odd...I thought I shut the door...

Cotton wool soaked in chloroform!... Snowy!... Kidnapped!

Snowy?...

SPLOSH

???... False alarm!

But where is Snowy?

I'll fix you, you vermin! I'll fix you!

OH!

Vermin!

Beast!

Snowy! My poor Snowy!... It's me... Don't be afraid...

YOW!

A rat!

NOW!

So, my clever friend ...
I...I...I'd like to... to explain ...

You don't need to... I do the explaining around here...
I assure you ... I mean... It was all a mistake...

The radio operator! My luck's in!... Sleeping Beauty, if you only knew...!

Aha! He's coming.

Snakes!!

Supposing it's...

SNOWY!

Murderer! You were going to drown my dog!
Your dog? What dog?

Dog?...Fog!...A foggy dog! Ha! Ha! Ha! Little dog laughed ...That's rum! Rum-te-tum! Fifteen men on the dead man's chest ...

?

Why not?...Rub it with camphorated oil!...And that's not all ... Sister Susie's sewing socks for soldiers!
He's knocked himself silly!

Here, come with me!
Only on condition that we go together...

It's getting rough!
Rough stuff! Haha!

Have you seen the heavenly twins? I can't find them.
They came on the bridge with me, then vanished!

THOMSON!...THOMPSON!

They must have been washed overboard!

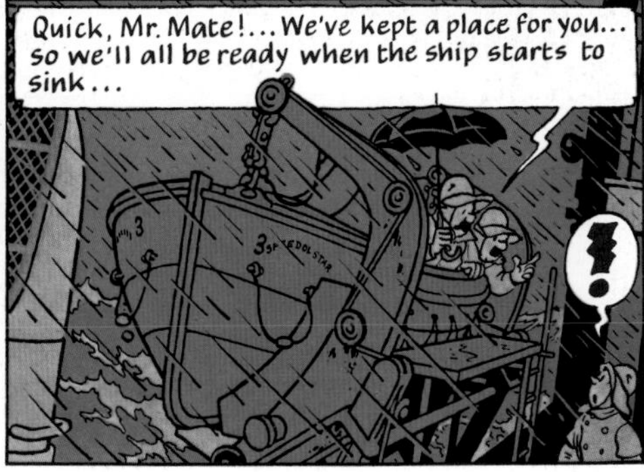
Quick, Mr. Mate!...We've kept a place for you... so we'll all be ready when the ship starts to sink...
!

Next morning...
Ah, the storm's blown it-self out...

How do you think he is?
No change... He's wandering...
Good morning... noon and night... light, fight, night... left, right, left, right.. pick 'em up, now!... How now brown cow?

No hope of learning any-thing useful from that quarter.

Several days later...
There's Khemikhal
Yes, and there's a launch putting out, with police aboard, I bet.

They've tightened up security... Only natural with the international crisis, and the tension in Khemed...

Military police: we have orders to search the ship.
Oh?... Very well...

Military police: this is a cabin search!
Go ahead.

Military police: open your bags!

Aha! As we were told: behind the coat-hooks!
!
?

These papers were hidden in the radio officer's cabin, sergeant.
Let me see!

Aha! All very interesting... A shipment of arms to Sheik Bab El Ehr!
I assure you, sergeant, I ...

Keep your hands off! ... We're police officers! We'll see you pay for this!
To be precise: you'll see we pay for this!

Heroin in their baggage, sir... And they're pretending to be police officers!
Indeed?

We were tricked, sergeant... An agent from Naval Intelligence gave us the package. He said it contained secret documents.
And where is this 'agent', eh ?

He's here on board, sergeant ... But he suddenly seems to have lost his wits...
Meaning that we can't question him, I suppose!... A neat little story... But it just happens that I am very far from losing MY wits!

What a fool I've been! ... Another false trail!

All right, get these three bright boys into the launch. They'll be interrogated ashore.
But...
I ...

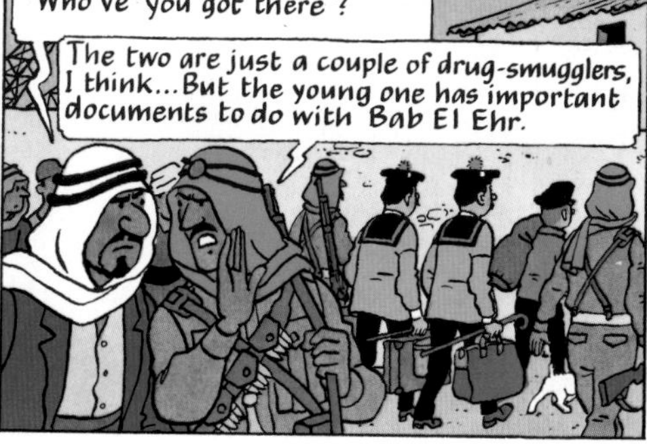
Who've you got there ?
The two are just a couple of drug-smugglers, I think... But the young one has important documents to do with Bab El Ehr.

Excellent work! Our noble sheik will reward you when he comes to power! ... Go now!

Bab El Ehr must be informed!

That evening . . .
I have come from Khemikhal, noble master. There I received news: the emir's soldiers have arrested a young foreigner.
Well ?

One of the guards works for us. He said he'd found papers on the prisoner... papers referring to an important shipment of arms for you.
The young man shall escape and be brought here to me !

Next morning . . .
Come with me. You're going to the special security gaol. The secret police want you for questioning.

There they are, Mohammed! Put your foot down!

Over here!

Hurry!

Meanwhile . . .
We've checked your papers. They're in order. You can go.
Thank you. What about Tintin?

Your friend ?... He was seized on his way here by Bab El Ehr's men.

Now we've got to find them ... And that's a thankless job. They made the snatch, and vanished without trace. Still, there's a £5000 reward for anyone who leads us to the sheik's hideout.

Five thousand pounds! You needn't say that again!... By this time next week we'll bring you Bab El Ehr trussed like a turkey!
Very good! May Allah go with you!

Next morning . . .
Five thousand pounds reward!
5433

Here is the young foreigner brought by your partisans, noble sheik.
Enter!

Greetings, and welcome, young stranger... Heaven will bless you for embracing our great cause... Now, when do the guns arrive?
What guns?

What guns? Our guns, our shipment of arms... You've brought news of their delivery: isn't that so?
Me?... Not me, most noble sheik! ...

You lied to me, son of a mangy dog!
Oh, no! most powerful master... It was the guard who told me... I swear by Allah!

That's quite true, noble sheik. Some papers were found in my cabin... but they didn't belong to me... And I've no idea who put them there...

It's a trick... A miserable trick to discover my hideout... I suppose you think I'll let you go?... To run home and betray us to the police, those snivelling lap-dogs of Ben Kalish Ezab? ...Never! You stay here with us. You are my prisoner!

?

Tie him up, and guard him well!
RRRRRRRR
A plane!

Noble master! A spy-plane from the emir!

That's the sheik's camp..

BANG
BANG
BANG

Poor fools, they're dropping leaflets... and none of my men can read! Hahaha!!

لعنك الله ... يا ابن الكلب يلعن ابوك بدوي
Such language! ... Don't listen to him, Tintin ... even in Arabic!

BANG
BANG
BANG

We strike camp at sunrise!... Before two days have passed we must be hidden in the mountains.

As for you, you come with us! You'll make a good hostage!

Meanwhile...

I say... Are you quite sure we're going in the right direction?
Of course I'm sure.

Anyway, we can't go wrong... They said drive straight on.
Quite right. And there's the first of our wells.

We'll stop there for a minute and fill the radiator.

?
?

Goodness gracious! ... A mirage!
A mirage?... Really?... I thought they'd been abolished.

Never mind: we'll drive on...

Ah! We've made good time. There's Tel El Esdi... We'll stop there for a drink...
Good idea!

Bother and... Another mirage!

And there's a third! They really are overdoing it!

We really are in a jam, and no mistake! ...

Next morning ...
There! All fixed now!

Off we go!

Look!
Ooh! ... A lake!

Why don't we have a swim!
That's a smashing idea!

I bet I can dive farther than you!
Show-off!

Fiddlesticks!...Another mirage!
To be precise: yes.

Meanwhile ...

Allah be praised!... See! The well of Bir Kegg!
Indeed!

Water!... At last!... I'm dying of thirst ...

A thousand curses! The well is dry!

No water! ... We must ride on!

?

The prisoner has fallen: he is finished!
Untie his hands: we will abandon him!

Wooah!... Wooah! ... Murderers! Rotten sand-hoppers!

You and your sense of direction! A fat lot of good it's doing us!
I tell you we're all right. This is a main road ...

I can prove it ... Look!
Pooh! Another mirage!

There you are! ... I told you so!

This time there's no mistake: we're saved!
My poor friend ... It's only a mirage ... Any fool can tell at a glance ...

No! No! I promise you it isn't!
It isn't, eh? ... Very well, I'll prove it ...

Whoops!

Oh ... my goodness ... I ... er ... I beg your pardon ... I mistook you for a mirage!
?

وقف عندك ،جبان
ملعون ،كسر راسك

You were absolutely right: it wasn't a mirage ...
No? ...

Meanwhile ...

He's coming round ... at last!
Where am I?... What happened?... Oh... I remember... The Arabs... crossing the desert... the dried-up well ...

The devils! They left me behind... We've got to get out of this somehow...

Many weary hours later . . .

There!... I can't believe it!... A pipeline... palm trees... an oasis! Look Snowy! We're saved!

If only... if only it isn't a mirage!

A well!... Water! ...Thank heavens! ... Water!

loving, loving water!

Meanwhile, some miles away ...

Hey presto! Another mirage!
You think so?... It looks real to me... If I were you I'd drive round it...

Me? Drive round something that's nothing but something you think is something but is nothing?... I never heard such rubbish!... We're going straight ahead!

To be precise: I told you so!

Aaah... That was marvellous!

Now, all we need is something to eat... I wonder ... Yes!

We're in luck! ...Those are date palms ...Let's see...

HUP!
What are you hoping for? A couple of pigeon pies?

Oh, Snowy! I'm so sorry!

It's getting dark...We'll have to spend the night here, tomorrow perhaps we'll be lucky enough to meet someone..
These things have certainly got bones, but I'd prefer a chop!

Time passes...
Brrr! It's freezing cold... If only I could get to sleep...

Ssh!... What's that noise?...
?

Horsemen!... Snowy, our luck's really in! We'll be rescued!

Hey, wait a minute... Horsemen? In the middle of the night? Perhaps we'd better stay hidden...

They're all dismounting...

Ahmed, you guard the horses... You two come with me!
Where have I heard that voice...?

What's going on?

Get on with it... and hurry!

What can they be doing over by the pipeline?

They're running back ...
I wonder if ...

?
BOOM

Great snakes!
They've blown up the pipe-line!

On your horses!... The alarm will be raised!
That voice!... I'm sure I know that voice!

Hello, what's that one doing?

Now I can see... He's fixing a stirrup or something ... Dare I ... ?

Come on, Snowy! ... It's all or nothing!
Heigh-ho! Now what's he after?

Where's Ahmed?... He isn't with us...

Ah, he's coming ... Ride on!

Meanwhile...
Hello... hello... pumping station twelve reporting total loss of pressure ...pipe must be broken above this station... Please send a repair-gang imme- diately...
I must be mad... This is crazy ... But it's too late now. I've taken a chance and can't turn back...

Hello... Hello... Pumping station eleven? ...Number one control here... Close all valves immediately... The pipe's fractured between you and number twelve ... A repair-gang is on the way ...

This is where we separate... It will confuse any pursuers... Ahmed will come with me...

Where in the world have I heard that voice?

Whoa!

Hold my horse... Wait here ... I'll be back in a moment ...

?

Crumbs! I know who that is!... It's Doctor Müller! (1)

What's he doing?

Where can he have gone?

CRACK
?

Poor silly Ahmed! Sometimes a mirror comes in handy to see what goes on behind you!... And I don't like spies!

But,...it isn't Ahmed ... Krutzitürken! It's Tintin!
Tintin?...What's he doing here? Something must have aroused his suspicions, but what? ...Perhaps I'd better wait till he comes round, then question him...No, that'd be useless-...a waste of time...

You've meddled in my affairs once too often, Tintin!...I'm fixing you for good!

Ach! What's that? It sounds like...It can't be ... Yes! It's a car...

No, a jeep!... Der Teufel! They're after me already!

(1) See The Black Island

The horses! If they spot the horses I'm done for!

What about Tintin? ...Kill him now?... No, they'd hear the shot... Ach, he's out cold; there's plenty of time to deal with him later...

So, they've gone! That was a close thing...

Quick! I must take care of Tintin... I was careless ... I should have bashed his brains out with my rifle butt...

Teufel!
!

BANG

Just in time!
BANG

BANG

BANG
BANG
BANG

What's all that racket?

BANG

Now what?... Any more?... No, it's all quiet: he's stopped shooting... Perhaps it's a trick...

Hey, what's that?... Galloping horses?... He can't have...

Yes! He's made off with both horses, the thug!

Here I am, back to square one... with a bump on my head as well!

On our way, Snowy... we haven't any choice...

We must follow his tracks!
Let me near that brute again and he'd better watch his trousers!

What's it all about?... What's that gangster Müller doing here? ... And why should he want to wreck the pipeline?... When he had me at his mercy, why didn't he kill me? ... I just don't have any of the answers.

Hello... I can't be mistaken... Let's take a closer look...
?

They're wheelmarks, Snowy... This really is a bit of luck!
Splendid!... Perhaps we're on a bus route!...

Let's see... I'd say they were tyres on a jeep... The sand and pebbles were thrown back by the wheels, so it was travelling that way. We'll go in the same direction...

And we'll worry about our friend Müller later.

Meanwhile ...
I don't like it, Thomson ... If we don't get somewhere soon ...

It's all right!... Look!... There! ... Tracks of a car!
Quite correct! And they aren't a mirage, either!

All we do is follow the tracks and we're saved!

An hour later ...
Hooray!... More tracks!... A second car joined the first one...

A real stroke of luck hitting this road.
To be precise: we've really had a stroke!

Another hour later...
There!... A third car joined the other two! ... We're on a very busy road...

Several hours go by...
Another one!... That makes the seventh.

We're obviously getting near a big town and ... Hey! Stop!... What's that there, ahead of us?

A can of petrol !

A full one too! ... That's lucky... for us, at least... Not for the poor chap who lost it.

I'd better check that ours is properly fixed: you can't be too careful.

!
Goodness gracious!

Us too! We've lost our petrol can! ... Look, the strap's broken !
Goodness gracious!

It must be somewhere behind us. Hurry up and turn round. We must go back and look for it.
I agree. Petrol is much too precious to lose.

Off we go... It can't be far.

An hour later...
Almost a motorway, Snowy!

A busy one, too. Look at the number of tracks. The marks are still fresh, too... Hello, that's odd... These tracks are all exactly the same... Could be a convoy of jeeps... Unless...
Unless what ?

Yes, it's only too obvious ... There's just one vehicle going round and round in circles, following his own tracks... The driver has lost his way, just like us ...

?

Oh, Snowy! Look! That's even worse! ... It's a sandstorm : The Khamsin!

Ooh! Here it comes! We're right in the middle of it!... Worst of all, the wind and sand will wipe out all the tracks...

This awful sand...gets in your eyes...and your mouth...We can't go on!...Only one thing to do...

Wait till the storm blows over...

Ssh!... I heard something...There it is again... A car engine!

We can't go on like this. We must raise the windscreen and put up the hood...

OOEE!

Ugh! this sand!

Careful! You mustn't let go...
Don't worry, I'm holding it.

OOEE!

Come on, Snowy!

Hang on tight! ... Don't let it get away!

OOEE!

OOEE!

?

What happened ?

Good heavens! A bowler belonging to one of the Thompsons!... How can they possibly...? Surely they couldn't ...?

Thomson!...Cooee!...Thompson!
Thomson!! Cooee!...It's me, Tintin!

...Ee...omson...Tin...in...
?

I say, did you hear anything? ...No?... I thought I heard someone over there, calling our name.
Come along, come along! It's just another mirage. Get in. We must move!

They've started the engine...They didn't hear me...
My gun!...A shot! They'll certainly hear that

BANG

Hooray! They heard me! They've stopped again.

Cooee!...Thomson!

Nothing!...The tyres this side are quite all right. Funny: I was sure I heard a loud bang.
All well this side... Right: on we go!

COOEE!... THOMSON!
... OMSON...
?
?

A mirage, my dear fellow... And not for the first time ...I can't think why you're still taken in by them... Come along!

The sound of the engine is fading...Too late...They've gone...

It's all over, Snowy ... We're done for...
Heigh-ho! That's nice!

I say ...
What?

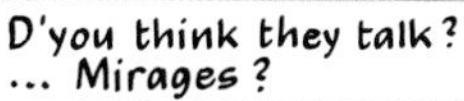
D'you think they talk? ... Mirages?
Talk?... Mirages? ... What a simple soul you are! Of course they don't talk. Mirages are seen but not heard!

Then what about those shouts we heard just now?
The shouts?...I... Goodness gracious! You're right: they weren't a mirage!... Quick! About turn!

?
The noise of an engine again! They're coming back!

BANG

Look!
Tintin!
It's them!

Found!... Found at last!... That's marvellous! I'm absolutely overjoyed ...
My dear old friend Thomson!

... to have my hat back!... What incredible good fortune!

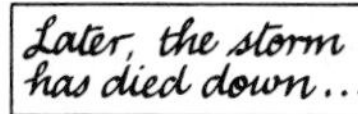
Later, the storm has died down ...

Poor Tintin, he was completely worn out. Look: he's fast asleep.
Zzzz Zzzzz

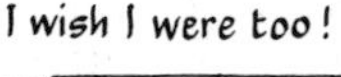
I wish I were too!

Yes, but this isn't the moment!

Zzzz Zzz
Zzzz Zzzz

Zzzz Zzzz
Zzzzz Zzzzz
Zzzzz Zzzzz

La illaha illallah!... Mohammed rassoul Allah! ...

!!?...
What... what happened?...
?

What happened?... Have you any idea?

Me?... No... I think I must have fallen asleep over the wheel ... I wonder what became of Tintin...

Next morning...

Well, Mohammed Ben Kalish Ezab, will you sign the contract?
No.

As your Highness pleases... I hope you will not come to regret your decision.

Regret? Do I interpret that as a threat?

هناك شخص يريد مقابلتك

Very good. I will receive him..

I'll get even with the old ostrich!

His Highness awaits you ... Follow me...
Whew! That was close! He didn't see me!

What's that gangster doing here? ...I must keep my eyes open!

Salaam aleikum, most noble emir Mohammed Ben Kalish Ezab...

Aleikum salaam, young stranger...Welcome to Hasch Abaibabi ...Be seated, and tell me what you wish of us...

It's like this, your Highness. Yesterday evening I was in a jeep driven by two of my friends. They arrived in the city...
This I know! The two men of whom you speak will be flogged: it is richly deserved!

Most noble emir, I have come to beg your mercy. For days and days these two men were wandering in the desert. They lost their way and were at the end of their strength. That is why...

I see, I see...It shall be considered... But tell me, what were they doing in the desert? And what are you doing here, dressed like the Bedouin? ... Explain...

Gladly, your Highness... But it is a long story and I fear to impose upon you.

No, no, I adore stories. You may begin. I am listening.

Two hours go by ...

At that moment there was a burst of flame: they had fired the pipeline.

Yes, it was one of two raids. I heard about them yesterday. There were two more last night. If only I could lay my hands on that mongrel Bab El Ehr!

So it's Bab El Ehr who ...
Yes, he's trying to depose me, with the help of Skoil Petroleum. Should he come to power he would lease the oil concessions in Khemedite Arabia to Skoil, and expel Arabex who operate with my agreement. That's why Bab El Ehr and his brigands attack the Arabex installations...

Now, the present contract I have with Arabex is soon due to expire. If I wished I could then sign a new contract, but with Skoil. That is the proposal made to me by Professor Smith who left here just as you arrived.
I think I understand.

It's very simple: if I sign a contract with Skoil the attacks will cease immediately. So why do I refuse to sign Professor Smith's contract ?
Yes, why, I wonder ?

It is strange, I do not know why I am telling you all this... You are a stranger... I have no reason, but I trust you. So... Inch' Allah!... I refuse to sign the contract because I do not like Professor Smith and I do not like his Skoil Petroleum.
Oh ?

But I have interrupted your story... You were telling how the saboteurs had blown up the pipeline..
They came running back and remounted their horses. I remained hidden behind the rocks ... Suddenly...

Master!... Master!... Oh! Master!
What is it ?... Who dares to disturb us?

Oh, Master! Master!... Your son!...
Well, Ali Ben Mahmud, what new prank is my little lamb playing this time?
Heaven grant that it is indeed a prank! Master, your son has disappeared!
Ha! ha! ha! ha!... Disappeared!... If you knew my son you would laugh as I do. He's the naughtiest young rascal anyone ever saw!... Every day he thinks up some new little wickedness ... But come with me, you'll see for yourself...

He was in the garden, Master...
Yes, yes, Ali Ben Mahmud, calm yourself!

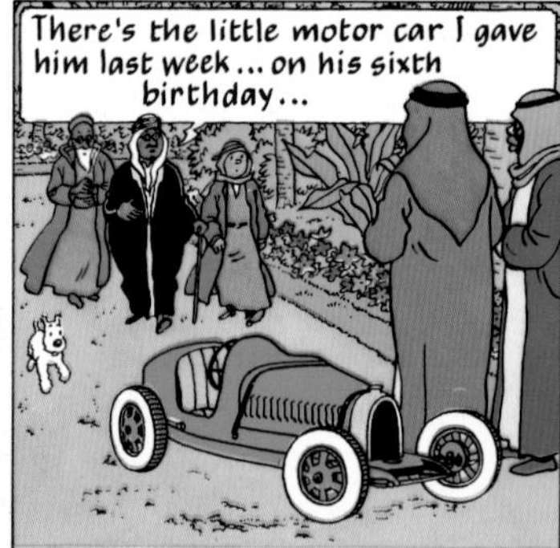
There's the little motor car I gave him last week... on his sixth birthday...

Abdullah!... Abdullah!... Where are you, my treasure ?
?

Abdullah!... Come out now, my little sugar plum!

Abdullah, my baby lambkin...

Abdullah!... Abdullah! Where are you hiding?

Abdullah, you little rascal, if you don't come at once Papa will be cross!
Excuse me, Highness, but does your son wear a blue robe ?
A blue robe?... Abdullah?... No! ... Why do you ask ?

Here's a piece of blue cloth I just found, caught on a branch ... Under the tree are some very deep footmarks... Obviously someone was hiding in the tree, and then jumped to the ground...

Perhaps... Yes... But...

There's your son's motor car... It has been shoved to one side, as you can see from the tyre marks...

But I don't understand... What are you trying to say?
I hardly dare tell you, Highness... I fear the worst... Come with me... There will be other clues...

There! I knew it!... More footmarks!...

And here... and there ... And look! Marks on the wall! This is where they must have climbed over...

They?... Who?
The men who kidnapped your son, Highness!

The men who... You're mad!... My son!... Kidnapped?... Why? ... Tell me why anyone should kidnap my son?... You're crazy!... You've made all this up! ... You're lying!... Yes, you're lying, like all infidels!...

Where is Mohammed Ben Kalish Ezab?
Over there, by the wall, with the stranger.

A horseman brought this letter, Master... Then rode away like the wind, out into the desert.

BY ALLAH!

It's unbelievable!... Here, read this letter...

?

Excuse me, Highness ... it is in Arabic...
Oh yes, I will translate for you...

"To Mohammed Ben Kalish Ezab... If you want to see your son again, throw Arabex out of Khemed." It's signed: Bab El Ehr.
Yes, it's what I would expect!

Bab El Ehr! Bab El Ehr! Son of a mangy dog!... Grandson of a scurvy jackal!... Great grandson of a moulting vulture!... My revenge will be terrible!... I will impale you on a spit!... I will roast you over a slow fire!... I will pull out your beard, one hair at a time... And I will stuff it down your throat...

But we must act! Where is my military adviser?

!
Ohhh!... His little car!

Boo-hoo-hoo-ooo-ooo ooo!... My little Abdullah! ... My little honeybun, where are you?... My little peppermint cream... Boo-hoo-hoo... hoo... hoo...
Highness, you must calm yourself..

Woo-hoo-hoo... My little angel... Boo-woo-hoo-hoo!

My little Abdullah! ...Aaaah... Aaaah ...Aaaah... Aaaah...
?

TCHOOO!... Aaa-ah...TCHOO!... Aaaah TCHOOO!

You see... Aaaah... TCHOOO!... It was one of his last tricks: he'd just found out about... Aaaah TCHOOO!... about Aaaah TCHOOO!... about sneezing pow-ow-ow-der!... He wanted a box for his birthday...

A few minutes later...
This is Yussuf Ben Mulfrid, my military adviser. He'll explain his plan of campaign... A cigarette?
No, thank you. I don't smoke.

Well, noble master... In two hours, three hundred horsemen will be ready to leave in pursuit of Bab El Ehr's followers. I have already given orders for scouts to follow their trail... Briefly, I can say to you...

PCHTT

Allah is good!... My little poppet replaced all my best havanas with his trick cigars... Wasn't that sweet?...

My one and only little chickadee!...

PCHTT

By the beard of the prophet! That wretched little centipede has changed all my best Sobranies for his filthy joke cigarettes!...

Two hours later ...

There they go... With Allah's help they will succeed... they will snatch my dear duckling from the hands of that monster, Bab El Ehr!

To tell the truth, Highness, that expedition is entirely useless... Useless, for the very good reason that Bab El Ehr didn't kidnap your son. We've got to look elsewhere for him...
?

What?! ... Not Bab El Ehr?... But you saw the letter he sent...
Yes, I saw it, Highness... But what proof have we that it really came from Bab El Ehr?... Would you recognise his writing?

His writing?... Actually, no... But... but if you knew it wasn't from him, why didn't you say so sooner? ... And another thing: why did you let me send out my horsemen?
Why?...

Quite simply, to make the real kidnapper believe that his trick has succeeded... Then, unless I'm very much mistaken...
The real kidnapper? ... You know who he is?

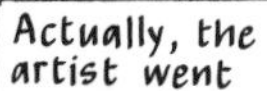
I think so, Highness, but I need more proof... And I don't know where he has taken your son... That's the main thing we've got to discover... By the way, have you a recent photograph of Abdullah?... It would be useful if I could have a look at it.

That's his latest portrait..

Poor little cherub ... The sittings were real torture for him ...

Actually, the artist went insane ...

Ah, let's see ... Is this one of those infernal cigarettes? ... No, it's a real one...

Papa begs your pardon, lambkin, for such a wicked suspicion!

Another of his confounded tricks! ... Now where did he get that ?

Well, he's certainly quite unmistakable! ... Now I must start my search, Highness ... Could you fit me out with some different clothes? ... And I'd like some information on Doctor Mül ... I mean Professor Smith.

Professor Smith? ... You think he can help you find my son? ...
Perhaps ...

He's an archaeologist, digging for remains of the ancient civilisations that once flourished in these lands ... At the same time he acts as representative for Skoil Petroleum.
He lives here?

Yes, in Wadesdah, my capital ... about twenty miles from here, on the coast. He lives in an enormous palace, perched like an eagle's nest on the top of a cliff.
I see ... There's just one more thing ...

BANG

Take no notice ... Just a cap ... Abdullah scattered them everywhere ... They livened things up in the palace ...
Oh? ... I see.

Where was I? ... Oh, yes ... The two friends I mentioned ... I have a great favour to ask on their behalf: please treat them as your honoured guests. Lavish every comfort upon them; take every possible care of them ... But if you want me to find your son, for pity's sake don't allow them out of the palace on any pretext whatsoever.

Next morning, in Wadesdah ...

That must be Professor Smith's palace, up there ...

!
ATCHOO!

A cold? ... Or sneezing powder? I'd better follow.
ATCHOO!

?
تفضل ....
صباح الخير

Great snakes! It's Senhor Oliveira da Figueira! (1)
تفضل سيدي
عندي كل ما تريد
وباثمان رخيصة

What a salesman! Just the same! He's persuaded that man to buy a pair of roller-skates!

انا تحت امركم
مع السلامة
ATCHOO!..

Nasty cold, eh?
Yes, a sudden epidemic ... started this morning among Professor Smith's servants...

But come in, come in, honoured sir... Absolutely no obligation ... But I'm sure you'll find a little something you need once you're inside my shop ...

To tell the truth, Senhor Oliveira, I don't need anything ... But I'm delighted to see you... Do you remember me?
Tintin!... Esplêndido!... What a wonderful surprise!... This calls for a celebration!

Si!... Si!... You must take a glass of wine with me... Some fine Portuguese rosé ... My country's bottled sunshine!

Now, what brings you to this god-forsaken land!

Well... I... I... er... I'm interested in archaeology...
Ah, like Professor Smith...
?

Exactly...You seem to know him. Tell me, what's he like? A pleasant sort of fellow?
To be honest, no; decidedly not. He's tough, and cruel, and ...

ZZING
BING
CRACK
BUMP

There's a mousetrap in the cupboard, but it sounds as if we've caught a full-grown rat!

?

(**1**) See Cigars of the Pharaoh

All right ?
There...yes...a big mouse for a small trap!

Excuse me... A customer ... I'll be back in a moment.
Please don't worry ... I'll clean up the mess while you're gone.

You see what happens to Nosey Parkers!

There, all tidied up... Hello, a radio. I wonder if I can get any news ?

CLICK

What's the matter ?... Dead ?... It doesn't even light up...

Oh, I see. The plug isn't connected.

There, it should work now.

WOOAAAH!
?

The wrong plug! Let's try this one...

Now...

Ah! My beauty past compare ... These jewels bright ...
!

... I wear ... Was I ever Margarita ? Come, reply...

WHEET... CRACK... CRR ...
dernières nouvelles d'Europe ... CRR ...
AA ?... AA ?...
HNET! ... HNET... CRR...
The European news service..

Following today's meeting of foreign ministers a spokesman indicated that there had been a definite easing of tension... An easing too of the outbreak of engine explosions which has bedevilled many countries. The epidemic seems to have ceased as mysteriously as it began.

In a statement, Mr. Peter Barrett, Head of the Fuel Research Division of the Ministry of Transport, told our reporter he had nothing to say, except that his department's investigations were continuing...

Here we are... Ah, you're listening to the news...
Yes, The threat of war seems to be lessening, thank heavens!

Now, what were we talking about?
About Professor Smith. You were saying that he isn't particularly likeable.

That's true... But he's extremely rich, and I'm his main supplier... So you see... My customers include all the top people in the area... At least, not quite all... Not the emir, alas!... What a man!... One of the best!... Which is more than can be said for his nasty little son... A real pest, young Prince Abdullah!... But you won't have heard: he's just been kidnapped!
I did hear of it!

Look here, Senhor Oliveira, would you like to be appointed official supplier to the Emir Ben Kalish Ezab?
Would I like it?... Of course! ... It would be the crowning glory of my career... But... what would I have to do?

Help me recover Prince Abdullah... To do that, smuggle me into Professor Smith's house ...
Professor Smith... What for? ... Well, if you like... It's quite easy... I go there each morning ...

The next morning ...
Salaam aleikum, Murad!
Aleikum sala... Tchoo!!

Who is the young stranger?
My nephew Alvaro... I want him to meet the palace servants.

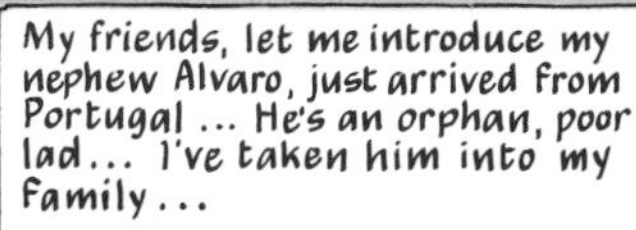
My friends, let me introduce my nephew Alvaro, just arrived from Portugal ... He's an orphan, poor lad... I've taken him into my family...

ATCHOO!

Just between ourselves he's a little ... well... a bit simple... Not surprising after what's happened to him... A dreadful story... Just imagine, his father, who was a well-known snail-farmer... Excuse me, just a minute...

Be a good boy, Alvaro ... While I'm busy with the gentlemen, you run and play in the garden... I'll call you...
Yes, Uncle.

But listen carefully, Alvaro ... Don't make a noise. Professor Smith is working in his study upstairs. You're not to disturb him ...
No, Uncle.

That's fine... He'll keep them safely occupied with one of his endless stories... but I mustn't waste time...

That'll be Professor Smith's study ...

Let's see if he really is there ... I just need some pebbles ...

Right on the shutters ...

Any sign of life?... No ...

Let's try again ...

RAT
TAT

No one at home ... Good!

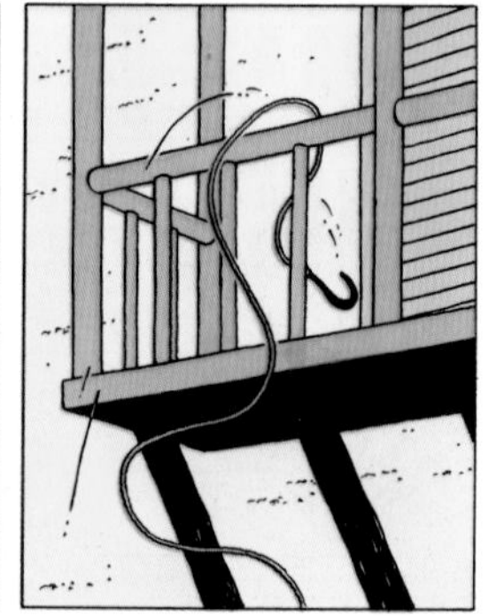

Hooked first time! That's a bit of luck!

There!... I made it!

Careful... mustn't take chances ...

Meanwhile ...
...So his father, who'd married the daughter of Da Costa the pirate from Lisbon, suddenly found himself in the middle of an extra-ordinary adventure. One day ...

Aha! ... The room's empty...

I must lock the door ... If someone comes, it'll give me time to make a getaway ...

?

The key's in the door... And the door's locked from the inside!... But there's no-one here... It doesn't make sense...

I'll work that out later... First, let's have a look at the papers on his desk...

What's in this folder?

Hello... A file of newspaper cuttings ...

SCIENTI
BAFFLI

MORE PETROL BLASTS
by our Motoring Correspo

WORLD'S AIRCRAFT GROUNDED
LONDON, Monday
Heathrow

FUEL MYSTERY
What's gone wrong with our petrol?
An outbreak of mysterious automobile explosions is terrorising the world's capitals. Car engines

Now why should Dr. Müller be interested in that petrol mystery? ... I wonder if ...

ATCHOO!
?!

Great snakes! The hearth is opening! ... I must hide! ...
Aaah...

TCHOO!

What's he doing in that corner?... Ah, I see... That's where a secret button for the trapdoor must be hidden.

Aaah... Aaah... TCHOO! ... Aaah ... TCHOO! ... Ach, that little pest! ...

Lucky I persuaded him to swap his confounded box of sneezing powder for a pair of roller-skates ...

There... I'll burn it in a minute ...

Drat! He's starting to write!

Let's hope he won't be long... I'm beginning to get pins and needles...

BZZZZ
BZZZZ
?

BZZZ
Ach!... A wasp!

Get away, you...!

Teufel! Just wait till I ...

Ah! There it is!

BZZZ

SNEEZING POWDER

Himmel! What have I done? ... Quick, the window... I must have air!

TCHOOO!

ATCHOOO!
?

That can't be an echo?... Aaah... I ... Aaah...

TCHOOO!
!

Come out... Aaah... Or I... Aaah... Or I'll shoot!
All right... Aaah ... I... Aaah... I'm coming...

Who... aaah... are you?... And what... aaah... are you doing there?
I... aaah... my name is ... aaah... Alvaro... I'm ... aah Senhor Oliveira's ... aaah... nephew... AAAH...

TCHOOOO!
TCHOOO!

Tintin!?
Yes, I...aaah...
Aaah...aaah...

This time, my friend, I'm making no...
aaah...
TCHOO!

?
AAAAH...

That's knocked him silly!... One more ...

AAAAAAAAH...
?

TCHOOO!

I'll break your rotten little neck!
!

I really have knocked him out this time!

AAAAH
TCHOOO!

Whew! Saved again! He's still out cold... Quick, I must tie him up, gag him, hide him somewhere... and telephone to the emir...

Meanwhile, in the kitchen...
...Alas! The poor woman never got over it. She died of grief and shame, at the age of ninety-seven. Her husband, broken-hearted, soon followed her to the grave. But that wasn't the end of the terrible tragedies this unhappy family had to suffer... One day, their son ...

There, Doctor Müller... That's taken care of you!

Hello?... Hello?... Is that the royal palace?... I want to speak to His Highness... Tintin ... Hello? is that you, Highness?

Tintin?... Yes... Where are you?... With Professor Smith?... What?... My son there?... A prisoner?... What's that you say?... What? ... Oh! You sneezed! Bless you!

You must send men to Wadesdah ... Have the palace surrounded... Meanwhile, I'll try to rescue the prince...

I can't say I like these toys, but this time I'd better be armed.

Now let's have a closer look at this...

?

Concrete tunnels! An underground fortress...

What's this?

A bunker...
...with gun ports commanding the town and the harbour...

Crumbs! What a place!... A real Maginot Line!

AAAAH...

TCHOOO!

Is that you, boss?
?

Boss?... Is that you, boss?
AAAAAH...

Nobody there ... that's odd ...

I could have sworn I heard a sneeze ...

Stop! ... Hands up ... or I'll shoot! ...
!

Don't move, and don't make a sound ... or else ...

Right! ... Now you're going to take me to the emir's son ... Get moving, and don't try any funny business! ... Understand ?

He's in there ...
You've got the key? ... Open up ...

All right? ... Stand away ... Face the wall, and keep your hands up ...

Quick, Abdullah! ... Hurry! ... I've come to take you home to your father ...

Shan't! ... Don't want to go home! ... This is a nice game ... Let me go! ... I hate you! ... I won't go!
But ...

BANG

Abdullah! ... Come along Abdullah! ... There isn't time to play about ...

?
اترك هذا

Whoopee! Clever me!
If only I...

You forgot this one, my friend!
Abdullah's got the key! Abdullah's got the key! Abdullah's got the key!

Abdullah! Now come along. That's quite enough!
NO!

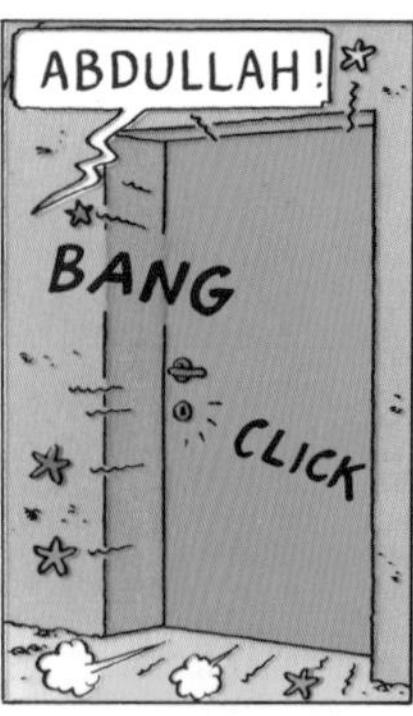
ABDULLAH!
BANG
CLICK

Abdullah, I... Confound it, he's locked the door...

Abdullah, for heaven's sake open this door at once!
WON'T

How in the world can I...

All right, I don't care. You stay if you want to. I'll go to the cinema without you, that's all... Goodbye!
Don't care!

TAP
TAP

TAP
TAP
TAP
TAP
TAP
?

ABDULLAH!
SHAN'T

?
WON'T

!
WAAAH! WAAAH! WAAAH!

Be quiet! For goodness sake!
!

YEOWW!

Be quiet, you little pest! Be quiet!
SHAN'T

WAAAH! WAAAH! WAAAH!

What about him?... I ought to tie him up, but...
WAAAH!

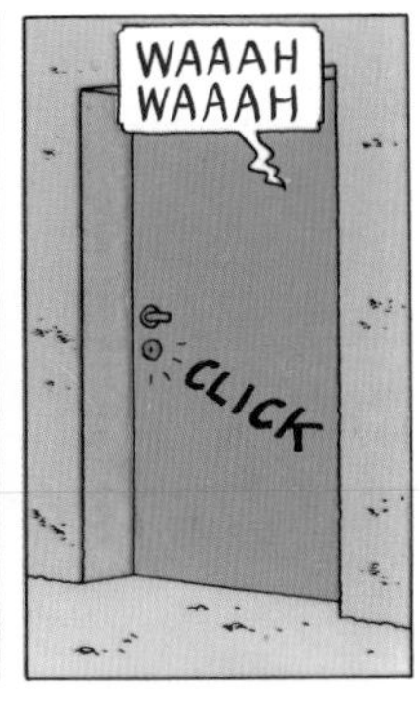
WAAAH WAAAH
CLICK

YEOW! YEOW!
WHACK
WHACK
WHACK
WHACK
WHACK
WHACK
WHACK
WHACK

I hate you!... I shall tell my papa!... And my papa is the emir!...
Oh yes...

Great snakes! He's come round... He'll raise the alarm, that's for sure...
?

...And my papa will have you flogged ...And then he'll have you impaled...
Good idea...

Quick, Murad!... Find Daud and Abdul... Take Daud with you and start searching from the far end... Send Abdul to me... We'll wait here for the young swine...
I go, master.

...At that moment the count stepped forward. Aha! he cried in Portuguese (you mustn't forget, Portuguese was his native tongue) and without a moment's hesitation he flung open the door... He stood frozen with horror!...

Daud!... Abdul!... Come at once!... The master needs you!

I... er... how I rattle on! I must go... an important appointment... Er... if you see my nephew, send him home, will you?... Goodbye!

With us here and Murad and Duad at the other end, he's trapped!

...And then he'll cut off your head... and play skittles with it... So there!

He can't escape... with the boss guarding the other exit...

Poor Tintin! What will become of him?

Hello, what's that?... It can't be... Why, yes, it's Snowy!

But we left him shut up in my house... How did he manage to get out?

Snowy!... Here, Snowy!

Meanwhile...
Ooh! Look! Over there... Rails! Rails to play trains with!
Yes, railway lines... But you can play later...

No!... Now!... I want to play trains!

Chuff-chuff chuff-chuff ...
Abdullah!

Abdullah!... Stop that!... Come here!
YEOWW!...

YEOWW!...
?

Chuff - chuff chuff - chuff...

Abdullah!... For heaven's sake, come back!
TOOOOT!

!
Get him, Abdul!

YEOWW!
RAT TAT TAT TAT TAT
RAT TAT

RAT-TAT-TAT
RAT-TAT-
RAT-TAT

OWW!
?
RAT-TAT-TAT

Quick, Abdul!

Stop him from closing the door!

!!!

RAT-TAT-TAT
RAT-TAT-TAT

Give yourself up!
Now your gun's empty ?! ... Just wait!

!
Nuts!...

Whew! That was close! But at least I've got a moment's peace!

?
PSCHH

Help!... Flares!... Supposing there's ammunition as well... ?!
PFTT
PFTT

PFTT
PFTT
PFTT
PFTT
PFTT
PFTT
PFTT
PFTT
PFTT

Seems to be calming down...

PFTT

That all?

BANG
This way!... Come on!...
?
RAT-TAT-TAT RAT-TAT
BANG
RAT-TAT

Tintin! Open up! Open up! It's me!
Snowy! It's Snowy!... And surely it can't be... that voice ... it's...
Wooah! Wooah!

Found you! Hooray!
Captain Haddock! ... And dear old Snowy!

PFTT

That's a friendly welcome, I must say!
Out! Quick! It's starting again!
PFTT
PFTT

All in the bag!... That's terrific!... How did you manage it?... And what are you doing here anyway, Captain?

Well, I'll tell you... It's like this ... Just imagine...
Sorry, Captain... First, have they found the emir's son?

I don't know... I haven't seen him... At least, not since I got here...
Quick!... Quick! We must look..

Is the emir there?
Yes, he was just now... I was going to tell you ...

There!

Tintin, Tintin! Everything is lost! We arrived too late... that fiendish professor escaped in a car... and he took my little duckling with him...
But someone's gone after them?

Yes, yes, of course... My horsemen are in hot pursuit... And your two friends with moustaches... in a jeep...
Oh dear! In that case ...

AHA!
?
?

Who does that car belong to ?
It's mine... Why ?...

Quick, Captain !...
!

Stop ! That's my car!... You can't have it !... It's mine !

Stop them ! Stop them ! They'll damage my car !

You're sure this is the way ?
Yes, it's the only possible road... But tell me, Captain... You still haven't explained how you come to be here...

It's quite simple really... but also rather complicated ...First, I must tell you...

Ah ! Look ! The emir's horsemen... That proves it ! We're certainly on the right track...

Forgive me, Captain... I'm sorry. I interrupted... You were saying ...

Well, as I said, it was quite simple and at the same time rather complicated... You remember...
Look ahead ! A cloud of dust !... D'you think it's Smith ?...

No, it's the Thompsons' jeep... We shall overtake them...

!
?

Hello, that's odd... I wonder why we...
What are you...

!

What on earth were you doing... getting out while we were moving ?

Moving? ... Were we moving? ... Oh, now I see ... It must have been that other car ... It passed us so fast I thought we were standing still ...

Meanwhile ...
L 11315

I'm thirsty!
So am I ...
I want an ice-cream!
Later, later ...

No! I want one now! I want an icecream! I want an ice-cream! ... Then I want to go home! ...

Shut up! There's your icecream!

Waaah! ... Waaah! ... Waaah! ...
And cut out that racket or I'll ... Sit down, Abdullah! ... Abdullah! Sit down here!

No! I want to sit here! ... I hate you! ... I shall tell my papa ... And my papa is the emir! ...
I know ... I know ...

?

Hee! Hee! My itching powder!

Yes, you're right ... I was just going to tell you ... As I said, it was really quite simple ... but at the same time rather complicated ...

There they are! Another dust-cloud! ... This time it's certainly Müller!

?

!

Great snakes! ... Smoke! ... What's happened to them?

Look at their tracks! ... Müller must have lost control of the car... it went over, and caught fire... Let's hope nothing's happened to the prince ...

Ooh! What a lovely accident!

Can we have another one ?
Ssh!... A car's stopping... Doors banging ... Wait! ...

All right, Müller... We've got you!
Aha! I've got a score to settle with him!

Got me?... Not yet!... Take one more step and I'll shoot the boy!
Whoopee! Just like a real gang-ster film!

Look! Another gun to shoot them with!
Thanks, Abdullah! You! Throw down your guns!

So you can shoot us down like rabbits?... No! We're keep-ing them!

Just as you like!... But watch it!... One false move and the child's had it!... Now, move away!... Go on, move back-wards...

Aha!... Excellent!... Another car ready and waiting!... Go on! Keep moving back!
Ooh! Papa's car! That's Papa's car! Are we going to play another accident?

Get inside, you! And keep your mouth shut!

Waaah!... Waaah!

All right... One bullet at the car when I go and I'll wring this repulsive little monkey's neck!... Understand?... So, auf wiedersehen!
Waaah! Waaah!

Beast!... Baby-snatcher!... Brigand!... Baboon!... Belemnite!... Bully!... Bougainvillea!... Bashi-bazouk!
Waaah!

I hate you! I'm going home to my papa!
Yes... Yes...

SLAM

Abdullah's jumped out!... Snakes! That makes a difference!
!

Quick, Captain!... Look after the boy...

BANG
BANG
!
BOOM

Müller, give in!
Never! You won't take me alive!
Wooah! Wooah!

BANG

BANG
BANG

They've taken cover... Only one chance for me... I must get round behind them...

You stay here with Abdullah and Snowy... I'll try to get round behind him... Any trouble, fire a shot... O.K.?
Fine...
I want to play with the doggie!
!

Be quiet, you miserable little sea-gherkin, you!
Waaah! I want to play with the doggie! Waaah!... Waaah!... Waah!

Bluebeard!

You duck-billed platypus!
Waaah!... Waaah!...

Now, thundering typhoons, you be quiet or I might start losing my temper!
Waaah! Waaah!

What's going on?... Where's Tintin now?...

It's too quiet... It's unnatural...

This silence bothers me... I'm sure something's brewing...

BANG
!

Billions of blistering barnacles!... You Arabian Nightmare!... I'll...

WHEET
BANG
BANG

Müller!... Over there!... Cunning swine! He was sneaking round behind... Lucky for us Tintin intercepted him...
BANG
BANG
BANG
Bang, Blistering-Barnacles! Bang!

Ach! Teufel! My gun's empty... Lucky I've got Abdullah's...

Müller!... Müller!... Look behind you... That jeep's full of police... And that other cloud of dust is a troop of the emir's horse... You're trapped, Müller!
?

The emir's horsemen!... He's right!... I'll be captured ...and handed over to that merciless fiend!... He'll torture me... put me on the rack! ... I'll be impaled... roasted on a slow fire... No! Never!

But first Formula Fourteen... I must destroy them... Where...?!... I must have lost them!...

Still, they don't matter now...

I told you I'd never be taken alive!... Now I keep my word!

Don't do it!... In heaven's name...

?

It was my ink pistol! I gave it to him, Blistering-Barnacles!

Driving in the sun has given me a splitting headache!
To be precise: I'm a headache too!

Hello! What's that there on the ground?

ASPIRIN

Aspirin!... What a stroke of luck!... One each, and our heads will vanish!

One...
Two!

Tastes a bit odd, I'd say...
Oh, you know, medicine is never particularly nice...

BHOOOP...
PHOOOP...

Blistering barnacles! ... Look at the two Thompsons!
Crumbs! Whatever's happened to them?

I don't know ... hic ... the heat, per... hic ... perhaps ... Unless it was the aspirin we ... hic ... we just took ...
A tube we found in the sand ... Here ...
What sort of aspirin?

I don't understand ... It seems real enough ... But let's take a look at the contents ...

Strange ... the tablets have the maker's mark, all right ... It's extra-ordinary ...
I agree, it's very odd ...

Blistering-Barnacles! Blistering-Barnacles! Look at your funny friends now! ...
!
?

Captain! Captain! ... How awful!
Er ... I ... hic ... feel rather peculiar!
Er ... to be pre ... hic ... Me too!
Do it again, thundering barnacles!

We must get help for them at once ... You take the car and return Abdullah to his father ... I'll drive the jeep, with Müller and the Thompsons ...
Hic ...
Right!

I'll make you rich for life if you destroy those aspirins, in-stead of analysing them ...
So! The tube belongs to you ... What's in the tablets?

Why worry? ... Destroy them and your fortune's made!
No thank you, Doctor Müller ... I'm not interested.

At Wadesdah Hospital, two hours later ...
Doctor, doctor! Come quickly! Two extra-ordinary cases! ...

There ...
!?

A little later...
Master!... See! Your car is returning! ...
With Abdullah?

With Abdullah!... Abdullah!... My little sugar plum!... My darling chocolate candy!
He can have his sugar plum, as far as I'm concerned!

My sweetest strawberry angel cake!...
At last! Now I can have a quiet smoke!
WAAAH!

Waaah! Waaah! Waaah! Want to stay with Blistering-Barnacles!

My nose!... Billions of blistering barnacles!... My nose!
Again!... Burn your nose again!
Come, come, don't be cross... It was his little game ...a jolly prank...

Ah, here comes Tintin...

So: the Thompsons are in hospital ... No one knows yet what's the matter... They have to have their hair cut every half hour... I sent at once to Professor Calculus, to ask him to analyse those filthy tablets, the ones Müller...
Müller?

Oh... of course, Highness... you don't know... Müller is the real name of Professor Smith.

That reptile! Where is he? Impale him instantly!

Müller is in the hands of the police, Highness. And I've given my word that he'll have a fair trial.
By Allah! How you Westerners complicate things!... We men of the East are far more expeditious!

The trial will attract plenty of attention! ... I found these papers on him. They prove Müller was a secret agent for a major foreign power... In the event of war it was his job to use his men to seize the oil wells, which explains the veritable arsenal we found under his palace... And he was already manœuvring to oust Arabex in favour of Skoil.

Those are the essentials. A police search of his palace, and a full interrogation of Müller and his accomplices will fill in the details. Quite simply, it's an episode in the perpetual warfare over oil... the world's black gold...

Some days later...
Tintin! Tintin!... A letter from Calculus!

My friends, I have immediately analysed the tablets you sent. I have discovered that if you add only a minute part to petrol its explosive qualities are increased to an alarming degree.
By trial and error I have concluded that one single tablet dissolved in a tank holding 5000 gallons of petrol would be enough to cause a

Anyway, Captain, that solves the mystery of cars blowing up... Hey, what's the matter? What have you got there?
Thundering typhoons!

Blistering barnacles! Look at that!
!

My house, by thunder! What's that nitwitted ninepin done to my beautiful house?!
Let's read on: he's sure to explain ...

... The research was exceedingly difficult. I enclose a photograph of Marlinspike after my first experiments ...
His first?... Did he do some more?!!

... Anyway, they were successful: that's all that matters. As for the phenomena in the capillary systems of the Thompsons, these will soon cease with the aid of the powders I have prepared and sent to you separately. The other substance I have sent is for use with petrol, and will entirely neutralize the effects of the compound Formula Fourteen...

Some weeks later...

"Each day of the Müller trial brings startling new disclosures. Today the whole mystery of the exploding car engines was revealed. It is now known that a major foreign power had developed a new chemical, known simply as Formula Fourteen. This chemical, added to petrol, increased its explosive qualities tenfold ..."

"In the event of war, the agents of this foreign power could easily contaminate the oil reserves of the other side. The recent outbreak of car explosions was by way of a trial, on a reduced scale, of this new tactic. Thanks to the work of the famous boy reporter, Tintin, the secret of Formula Fourteen has been discovered..."

"...An effective antidote has immediately been developed by his distinguished colleague, Professor Cuthbert Calculus, to neutralize the effects of the chemical. By his prompt action, Tintin has undoubtedly prevented the outbreak of war. Better news too of the detectives Thomson and Thompson who inadvertently swallowed some Formula Fourteen. They are now out of danger, and well on the way to recovery."

What about that? We had a narrow escape, eh?... If it hadn't been for the Thompsons, we'd be at war!... You know, Captain, you still haven't told us how you came to be mixed up in this business...
Oh, yes... Well, I... thank you, Highness...

Well... Pff... It's like this... Pff... I think I told you... Pff... it's quite simple really ... Pff... and at the same time rather complicated...

Would you believe it... Pff... I... Pfff...

!
PSHTT

Another of Abdullah's little tricks! ... And he promised me he'd be good! ... Ah, what adorable little ways he has!

Adorable!... Adorable!... I'll say he is!! ... Well, if you want to hear my story, it won't be from me!... Blistering barnacles, as far as I'm concerned, this is the end!

END

HERGÉ

THE ADVENTURES OF TINTIN

DESTINATION MOON

Destination Moon

DESTINATION MOON

Ah! It's the master!... And Mr. Tintin! How good to see you home again!
Hello there, Nestor!

I hope you are well, sir... Did you have a good trip?
Fine, thank you Nestor. All well?... I see the house has been painted... How is Professor Calculus? I'm looking forward to see- ing him.

Professor Calculus?... Hasn't he written to you?... He left here three weeks ago...
Calculus has gone?

Yes sir... Three weeks ago a gentleman with a foreign accent came to see Professor Calculus. They had a long talk. Then the Professor packed his luggage and they went away, together. He said he would write to you... I'm very surprised he hasn't!
Well I'm...!

RRING

Hello?... Yes... No, this is Captain Haddock... No, he's not here... Who is that speak- .. No, he left three weeks ago.. But who's speaking? ...Hello? Hello?..

Hello?... Hello?... He's rung off... the nitwit talked double-Dutch!... Hello?... Hello?... No, he's gone.
How odd!... Anyway, I hope nothing has happened to Professor Calculus... Shall we have a look round his room?

When I went in this morning to air the room, I noticed nothing unusual.
We'd better look...

GRR ... GRR
Look at Snowy!

Careful!
GRRR

?

Snowy!... Here, Snowy!

DING DING DING
?

No, there's nothing unusual in his room... What is it, Nestor?

A telegram for you, sir.
For me? Already? Who knows I'm home?
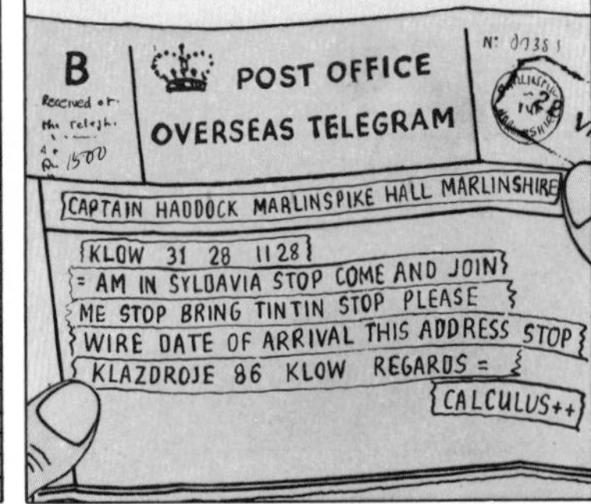
B
POST OFFICE
OVERSEAS TELEGRAM
CAPTAIN HADDOCK MARLINSPIKE HALL MARLINSHIRE
KLOW 31 28 1128
= AM IN SYLDAVIA STOP COME AND JOIN
ME STOP BRING TINTIN STOP PLEASE
WIRE DATE OF ARRIVAL THIS ADDRESS STOP
KLAZDROJE 86 KLOW REGARDS =
CALCULUS++

In Syldavia!... Calculus is in Syldavia!... What's the crazy fellow doing there?
It's very odd. He asks us to join him. ... Shall we go?

Of course!... No need to take the bags upstairs, Nestor. We're leaving at once.

Two days later...
SYL

You've read this brochure on Syldavia?... What a country! ... They export mineral-water, the poisoners!... I say, you're very preoccupied. Is something wrong?
Why did he promise to write, and then not do so?

He wired us: it comes to the same thing.
I'm not so sure. What proof have we that he sent the telegram?... Then, remember that mysterious telephone call?... Perhaps someone wanted to get us out of the house...

Blistering barnacles, it's true!... I hadn't thought of that!... He's quite a character, our friend Calculus!
?

Your whisky, sir...
Ah, that's very kind.

Stop, woman! Don't do that!
?

What are you doing?... Not one drop of that disgusting mineral-water in my whisky!

Two hours later...
SYL

Klow, ladies and gentlemen. Please fasten safety belts.

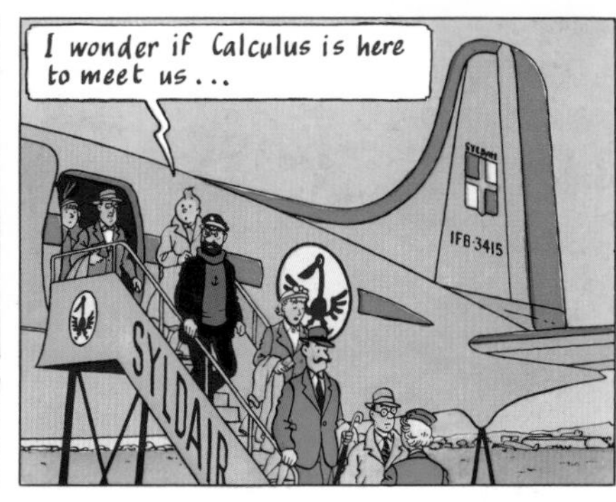
I wonder if Calculus is here to meet us...
IFB-3415
SYLDAIR

No, I don't see him anywhere... He must have received our telegram by now. Well, we shall see. Here we are at the Customs. Anything to declare, Captain?
Me?... Nothing at all!

And this?... Spirits!... There's a heavy import duty, zir. Only mineral-water here in Syldavia...

875 Khors import duty! Bunch of pirates! In our money that'd be...
Strange... I don't see Calculus...

All passports, please.
You Captain Haddock?... And him Tintin?
Yes.

Your friend... er... not able to come... he send car... You please come with me...
Oh, Calculus has sent a car for us. That's kind of him... Good: we'll follow you.

Wait... What about our luggage?
Already in the car, zir.

Take a good look at those two... They're joining the Mammoth. You see, Zepo have picked them up already...

Calculus is doing things in style, eh ?... With a chauffeur and a flunkey, by thunder !
Maybe...

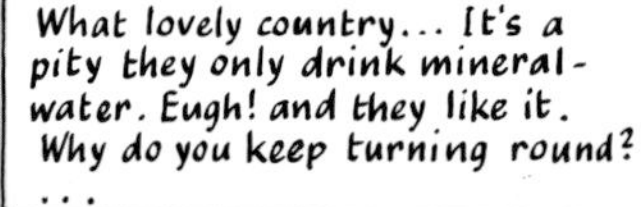
What lovely country... It's a pity they only drink mineral-water. Eugh! and they like it. Why do you keep turning round? ...

I'm watching that car... It's been following us from the airport ...
I expect it's going to Klow, like us.

Perhaps... Anyway we'll soon be there... We're coming to a town.

Hi! What's happening? We're not on the Klow road!
TESZNIK
TESZNIK
КЛОВ
KLOW
7,5

Hey, driver what's the meaning of this?... Where are you taking us?
?
Sprodj!

Sprodj yourself, you Bashi-bazouk! You were asked where we're going. Tell us!
Sprodj, zir. Your friend there...

ЮЕРХВЕН
ВЕРТЗРАГЗ
SLOW
ROAD WORKS

?

Billions of blistering barnacles! Why didn't you slow down, ectoplasm!
You speak me, zir? ... I not see.. we go...

Two hours later...
That other car is still following us...

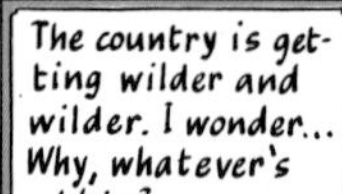
The country is getting wilder and wilder. I wonder... Why, whatever's this?

Captain, just look at that signboard.
ФОРВОТЗЕН
ЗОНА
SECURITY
AREA

By thunder, I'm thirsty! I'm going to get a drink... And while I'm about it I'll see just what that car's doing behind us.

Hält!... Ihn dzekhoujchz blaveh!

What?... Is this how you treat tourists in this thundering country of mineral-water-drinkers?
?

Thundering typhoons, I'm thirsty ... Thirsty! You understand? No? Er... J'ai soif... Ich bin durstig, blistering barnacles! Drink.. glug-glug
Ah?... Döszt?

Vladimir!... Eh! Vladimir! On fläsz Klowaswa vüh dzapeih.. Eih döszt!...
Ah, he's understood... About time too!

Billions of blue blistering barnacles! Mineral-water! And you think I'll drink a single drop of that nauseating liquid?

?

Sea-gherkin!... Pirate!... Logarithm!... Ectoplasm!... Baboon! You call yourself a policeman and you can't open a bottle properly!

Captain, come on! We're going!

Tribe of Polynesians!
ФОРВОТЗ ЗОНА • SECURITY AREA

Half an hour later...

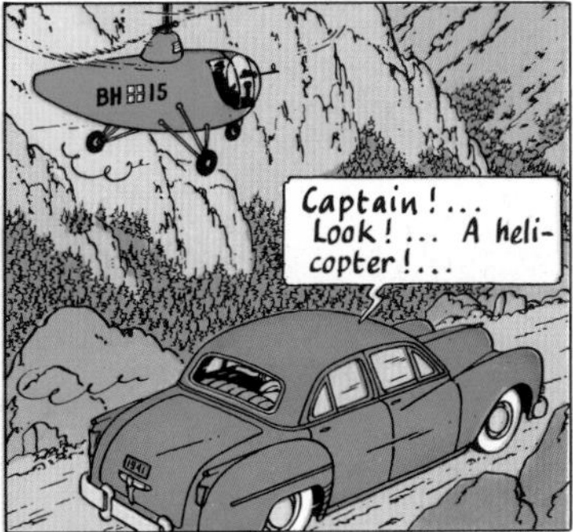
Captain!... Look!... A helicopter!...
BH 15

By thunder! It's landing in the road!... Here, Sprodj, what does this mean?
Check-pozt, zir.

Another check-point?

Güdd... Zrädjzmo... Zsālu endzoekhoszd.

Well, it's the first time I've ever seen that ...It's incredible! A flying check-point!

B.H. 15 calling Control... B.H. 15 calling Control... Expedition "Bluebell" passed check-point... All in order...

What's all this checking business? Where are we, and where are they taking us?
That's what I'm wondering.

Look, a house!... Here, Sprodj, is this where our friend Calculus lives?
Yes, zir...

What's possessed him to come and nest up here? I simply... Blistering barnacles! Another check-point!

Thundering typhoons! What's going on in this country? Anyone would think there's a war on!

And now that baboon's gone off with our papers! What's he doing with them?

P.K.1 calling Control ...P.K.1 calling Control... Expedition "Bluebell" has arrived... All in order... Open the doors...

Güdd!... Zrädjzmo!... Zsoe gnounh dzoeteuïh ebb touhn...
Ah, all's well ...We can go on.
Güdd!

Thundering typhoons, what's happening? Are we driving straight into the garage? ...That's an odd sort of welcome!

?
?

The doors have closed automatically behind us!

And the other doors are opening automatically in front!

Here you are, gentlemen.
A SECTOR
B

At last! And it's about time too!

Blistering barnacles! When are they going to make a car that you can get out of without cracking your skull?
Mr. Tintin?... Let me introduce myself: Frank Wolff, assistant engineer to Professor Calculus.
How do you do.

How do you do... But I'd like to know where we are... And what these gangsters are who followed us from the airport...
Gangsters, Captain? These are ZEPO men!

Zepo?... What sort of creature is a Zepo?
You'll see, Captain. Professor Calculus will explain everything. Come: he's waiting for you.

Fifth floor. We'll take the lift.

After you, gentlemen...

?
WOOAH!

Oh! I'm sorry. I didn't notice your dog!

1
2
3
4
5
Here we are...

This is where Professor Calculus works...

?
!
?

?
!
What is it?
Who on earth...

It's my dear old friend, Captain Haddock ..!

I'm so sorry! I completely forgot my helmet... It's a new model in multiplex; we were testing it for strength...
Believe me, it's strong all right!

A multiplex helmet? What for, may I ask?
No, no, no, no, it's not glass... Multiplex... Glass isn't nearly tough enough...

Of course... But what's this multiplex helmet meant for?
Certainly, certainly... Just a moment...

What did you say?
Ah, you're using an ear-trumpet now! But why not a hearing aid - one of those little instruments fitting into the ear? They're almost invisible.

Oh yes, I know what you mean... But they're meant for deaf people...

...and I'm only a little hard of hearing in one ear...

Now look, Mr. Hard-of-Hearing, when am I going to get an answer to my question: WHERE ARE WE?
Didn't Mr. Wolff tell you?... Well, I'll explain...

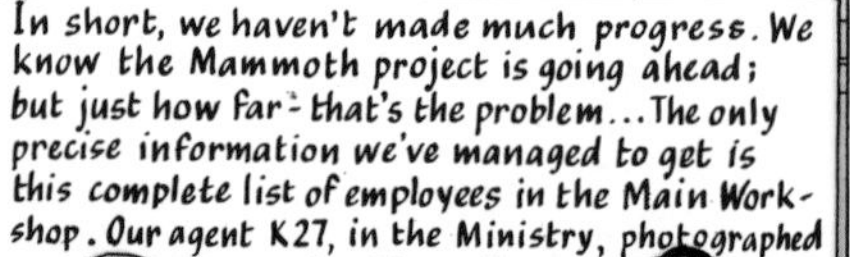

Meanwhile in Klow...

In short, we haven't made much progress. We know the Mammoth project is going ahead; but just how far - that's the problem... The only precise information we've managed to get is this complete list of employees in the Main Workshop. Our agent K27, in the Ministry, photographed it on microfilm. Here...

K.27 has not wasted his time, my dear Baron...

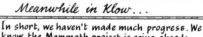

Come in here: I want to show you something...

Well, what do you think of it?
What on earth is that??

That, Captain, is a part - and only a part - of the Sprodj Atomic Research Centre.
An atomic research centre in this land of savages?

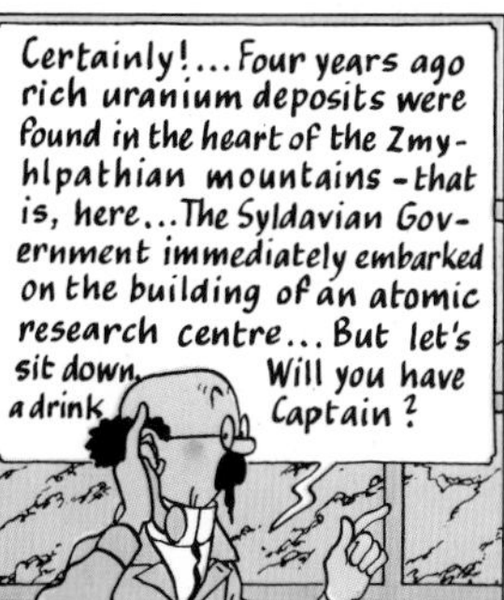
Certainly!... Four years ago rich uranium deposits were found in the heart of the Zmyhlpathian mountains - that is, here... The Syldavian Government immediately embarked on the building of an atomic research centre... But let's sit down. Will you have a drink, Captain?

Specialists in nuclear physics were recruited from many countries, and work began. It goes without saying that all the research is for humanitarian purposes... No question of making atomic bombs here... In fact, we are seeking a way to protect mankind from the dangers of these weapons...

Then the Syldavian Government invited me to work here. I have been put in charge of the astronautical section, as that is the field with which I am most familiar...

I have been very ably supported by my engineer, Frank Wolff. You met him earlier. And I'm just completing plans for a nuclear-powered rocket in which I propose to land ON THE MOON...

Ha! ha! ha! ha!... The Moon!... Old Calculus on the Moon! Ha! ha! ha!... The things you think of!... The Moon!... That's a good one!...

Ha! ha! ha!... The Moon!... As easy as pie!... A man on the Moon!... You'll be the man in the Moon!... Ha! ha! ha!

Oh! ho! ho!... I haven't laughed so much for years!... On the Moon!... And he's quite serious about it!... You old humbug, Calculus!

Here's to you!... Ha! ha! ha! Passengers for the Moon, all aboard the bus!... Sorry, the rocket!... You are taking passengers, I hope?

Of course!... Why else do you think I asked you to join me?...
!?
!

Eh ?... What ?... What are you saying ?

Me ?.. On the Moon!... With you ?... Blistering barnacles! your brain's gone radioactive! On the Moon!... You'd just push me around, like that, without a word!... On the Moon!!! I'll never set foot in your infernal rocket, d'you hear me ? Thundering typhoons! ... Never!
Oh, thank you, Captain... thank you!... I knew I could count on you.

Good evening, gentlemen.

Ah, Mr. Baxter. May I introduce Captain Haddock ? Mr. Baxter, the Captain is most enthusiastic. He says he and our good friend Tintin will be delighted to travel with me to the Moon.
Excuse me ... I ...
How do you do, Captain. The best of luck! The Professor told me that you were a man of remarkable capacity: I see he wasn't exaggerating.
Mr. Baxter is the Director General of the Centre
But I ...

No, no, don't be modest: a character such as yours is rare, all too rare... I congratulate you, and I envy you. ... You will have a unique privilege: the first man to set foot on our great satellite the Moon!

I congratulate you too, young man. In this perilous venture you will represent the eager spirit of youth. That's splendid...
Yes...er... No... I mean...

But it is getting late, gentlemen, and you've had a tiring day. We'll show you your rooms, and tomorrow the Professor will take you round the Centre... This will be the first time outsiders have been admitted... As you can imagine, we cannot be too careful about spies and saboteurs ...

Night falls. All is quiet. Down the long, silent corridors, guards are on patrol...

SB
C.32

Patrol 14 calling Control... Nothing to report...

All the same, "They" go a bit far... This inspection is absurd.. Who could possibly get in here ?...

By St. Vladimir!

Patrol 14 calling Control!... Patrol 14 calling Control!... Emergency!... Dense brown smoke filling corridors in H Sector... Send security squads at once!

Control calling Security... Emergency! Dense smoke reported in corridors, H Sector...

RRRING
RRRING
RRRING
RRRRRRRING

RRRRING
RRRRING
RRRRING
Zzzzz
Zzzzz
Zzzzz

RRRRRRING
Professor! Wake up, Professor!... The alarm bell!...
Time to get up already?

What's happening?
Fire!... All out!
Well, this is a fine start!...

This looks serious...
All out!... All out!

Ah, there's Professor Calculus...

Hello Tintin. What a to-do! Dreadful!... What did you say?
?
!
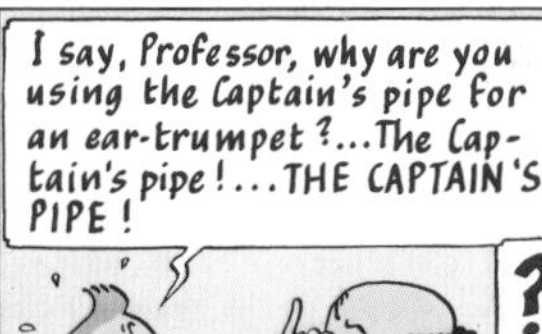
I say, Professor, why are you using the Captain's pipe for an ear-trumpet?...The Captain's pipe!...THE CAPTAIN'S PIPE!

?
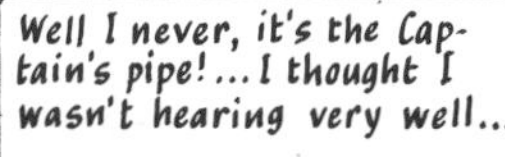
Well I never, it's the Captain's pipe!...I thought I wasn't hearing very well...

It's in here! Quick, use the foam.

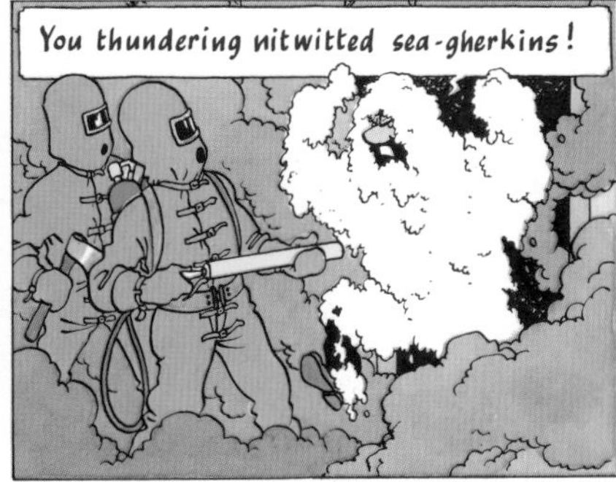
You thundering nitwitted sea-gherkins!

You Polynesians, you! You've been smart, haven't you? You Ku-Klux-Klan! Just when I was putting it out myself...
Putting out what?

This confounded ear-trumpet! I filled it and lit it, thinking it was my pipe. It started to burn: no flame: just this blistering smoke!
Oh I see: it's made of ebonite!

The next morning...
The Professor asked me to give you this... He's rather busy himself this morning, so he suggested that I take you round the Centre... You'd better put on these over-alls; then you can go round without being stopped continually by ZEPO.
?

The Zepo again?... Look here, just what is a Zepo?
The ZEPO?... ZE-PO... Zekrett Politzs... They are the special police responsible for guarding the atomic area, for anti-sabotage precautions and for counter-espionage.

On that score the ZEPO have plenty to do... Despite all our precautions, certain powers know that we are building a moon-rocket and their spies are actively interested. Happily for us they can only succeed if they have inside men. And even these would have to be senior staff... But we need have no worries about that... Now I'll leave you to put on your overalls.

Meanwhile...
Send this in code, my dear Baron: "A.K.R.12 to N.W.3. R. In contact at top level with Main Workshop..."

We are now in the central laboratories where the natural uranium - which comes to us in thin metal rods - is converted into plutonium... Plutonium will be used to power Professor Calculus's rock-et.

There are two principal stages in the production of plutonium: first the "cooking" of the uranium rods in the atomic pile which you will see in a minute; then the chemical extraction of the plutonium produced in the rods by the "cooking"... You follow me?
Of course!... I'm right behind you.

Through this entrance is the bay housing the atomic pile... Have your passes ready.

That's that. Now we'll go and put on the special clothing to protect us against radioactivity... By the way, with his usual thoughtfulness Professor Calculus remembered your dog; he's had a suit made for him - just the right size.

There... Now we can go in...
I know it's very good of Professor Calculus; but he must have measured a St. Bernard!

!
Look...
?

This is the atomic pile, made of enormous graphite blocks through which run aluminium tubes. The cadmium rods that you see right up there are plunged into the container which is surrounded by a thick concrete shield. Those huge pipes convey water to cool the plant.

It's incredible!... Terrific!

Isn't it? But come over here; it looks even more impressive ...
It's fantastic!

Stupendous!... Fabulous!... It... er...

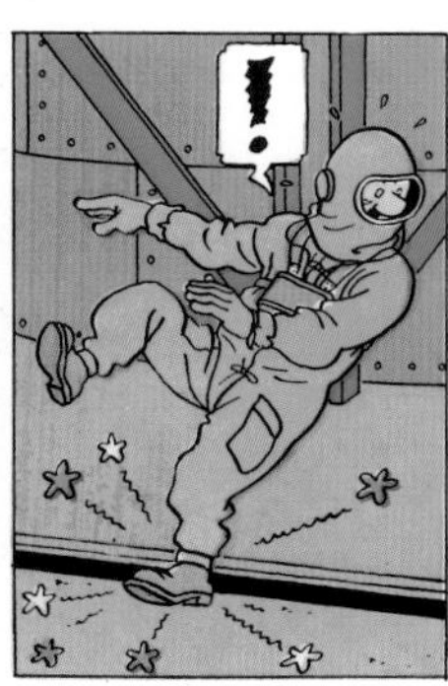

!

Bowls you over! That's what you were going to say, wasn't it, Captain?

I hope you aren't hurt?...
Hurt?...Oh no! ... Nothing at all!

Good. Now, back to the pile again. At this moment they are putting in a rod of uranium: uranium containing about 99% of U.238 and only 1% of radioactive U.235. Now what happens once the uranium is inside the pile?

Well... When an atom of U.235 splits, it releases two or three neutrons. One or other of these will be absorbed by an atom of U.238, which will thus be transmuted into plutonium ... But those other neutrons?... Where will they go?...
Yes... I'm worried about them...

Restricted by the graphite that surrounds them, they continue through the pile, and end up by hitting one of the rare atoms of U.235. These in their turn split and release two or three neutrons again... You see?
Of course! It's child's play...

But this process has to be controlled. Thanks to the cadmium rods which absorb a proportion of the neutrons, we can regulate the working of the pile as we wish.

Attention please! Attention please! Engineer Frank Wolff please contact Professor Calculus immediately!
?
!

Hurry! Something serious must have happened!

Hello!... Hello!... Professor Calculus?...This is Frank Wolff... You... How,.. What? ...The plans?... Gone??... Yes, we'll come at once.
?

You heard?... They're the detail drawings of an experimental rocket ... It's incredible! The Professor put them in his safe last night... This morning the plans are gone!... And only three people know the combination of the lock: Mr. Baxter, the Professor, and myself... Quick, we must go to him...

Just when is someone going to let me out of this fancy-dress?

A few minutes later...

And this morning when I opened the safe, look what I found: old newspapers instead of the plans...
?

We'd never hear the end of it if I rummaged in a dustbin! You'd do better to let me out of this duffle coat with a windscreen!

Excuse me, Professor, I may be mistaken, but I found these in the waste-paper basket. Aren't they the plans you're looking for?
Well I never!

I... Why, so they are!... But how could I? I'm terribly sorry... In a moment of absent-mindedness last night I must have put the plans in the basket, and locked up these old newspapers...

How lucky to have found them! These are plans of an experimental rocket we are just getting ready. Come, I'll show you... It's a model of the rocket which will, one day, take us to the Moon...

As you know, the Moon travels round the Earth, always showing the one face. The other side is completely unknown. The radio-controlled rocket we are going to launch will circumnavigate the Moon...

... and take photographs of the other side – the face which is, and always will be, invisible from the Earth. If only from the point of view of astronomy this will be of tremendous interest. But that is not our only objective. Needless to say the rocket...

... X-FLR 6, as we have called it, will carry a full range of instruments. When these are recovered they will give us invaluable information for our own trip to the Moon...

Look, there's X-FLR 6...

HALT!

What's that dog doing here in protective clothing?... You know these suits are not allowed in this sector.
Heavens! I quite forgot!

I'll go back with him. Here, good dog; come with me...
You may say that X-FLR6 is no different from other rockets already launched... But my reply to that is: our rocket's unique because it's the first...
Follow the gentleman, Snowy.
It's about time someone took an interest in me!

...to be driven by a nuclear motor ... And I, Professor Calculus perfected it!... How does it work? ...Well, think of a nuclear bomb: but instead of an instantaneous explosion, the force is spread over several days.

Of course, for launching and landing we shall use another engine, a simple jet, using a mixture of nitric acid and aniline...Why?... Because if we used the nuclear motor then, the radioactive blast from the exhausts ...
...would be a frightful hazard at the launching and landing sites... You may argue that the intense heat engendered by the nuclear fission would melt the motor itself! No! Because I have invented a new substance, calculon. It has a silicon base, and can resist even the highest temperatures. Thanks to these two inventions - the nuclear motor and calculon - we shall soon set foot on the Moon.

Ah, the very thought of it makes me walk on air...

Look out!

LOOK OUT!
CAUTION! WET PAINT

?

CAUTION! WET PAINT

A week goes by. Then, one night...
Radar to Control! Emergency!... Aircraft from South violating Security Area!...

Attention please!... Control calling!... Emergency!... Aircraft from South violating Security Area... Fighters and A.A. personnel to action stations

Sprodj Control to unidentified aircraft. Are you receiving me?... You are violating a Security Area... If you proceed you are liable to be forced down ...

They've spotted us!... They're ordering us to turn back!
At all costs don't answer them: we aren't over the right place yet.

Sprodj Control to unidentified aircraft. I repeat, if you do not clear Security Area, we will open fire.

We hadn't bargained for this! They say they'll shoot!
Answer with a few odd words to make them think we're in trouble... We must play for time...

... craft... F... R... receive... lost... course... please... our... posi...

A plane must have lost its way. Their radio is intermittent. They're trying to answer us. What shall we do?

This is it! Jump!

Radar to Control!... Three parachutists have just jumped from the plane!

Control calling! ...Order the Ack-Ack to open fire!

BOOM BOOM BOOM
Crumbs! It wasn't a dream: that's Ack-Ack fire!

HUUUUUUW
That's an unexploded shell coming down!

Zzzzzzz... Zzzzzz...

BANG

Great snakes! It went off in the Professor's room! Quick! I must hurry!
?

Who is it? Did someone knock?

Next morning...
Attention please! All personnel in category "A" please report at once to Mr. Baxter for an important announcement..
Category "A"?... That's us!
Yes. Come on!

Gentlemen, there have been serious incidents during the night... An unidentified aircraft flew over the Security Area. It eluded our fighters and anti-aircraft fire, and dropped three parachutists. The parachute of one failed to open and he was killed. His body was found this morning. He was carrying rations, arms, and a radio set, but of course no identification papers...

Till now the other two parachutists have evaded capture. Needless to say everything is being done to find them. They will undoubtedly be caught forthwith. Meanwhile, gentlemen, I ask for your co-operation...

Operation?... Who's he talking about, having an operation?... Is somebody ill?
?

... and would like to impress on you, my senior executives, the need for constant vigilance. This daring raid proves that even the strictest precautions cannot stop desperate men.

Thank you, gentlemen, that will be all. May I just have a word with the X-FLR6 team...

Perhaps your ear-trumpet is blocked?
Not in the least: it's just blocked, that's all.

You see? It's plaster... from that explosion last night... No, it won't come out like this...

Let's see, perhaps if I shake it...
Well, Professor, what are you up to now?

OH!
!
Blistering barnacles! I thought that sort of thing only happened to me!

I'm terribly sorry...
Don't mention it!

Excuse me: the telephone...
RRRRING

Hello... Yes... What?... Captured the parachutists?... Both of them?.. Splendid!... Greeks, you say?... That's odd. Bring them here immediately. I'll question them myself.

A few minutes later
...You've got the strong end of the wick... no, I mean ...
Silence!
RAT TAT TAT

To be precise: the stick!
These are the two birds, sir.
?
This is it!... Sensational appearance of the Thomson twins!

So the game's up, eh, my friends?.. You can start by explaining this get-up...
Get-up? You call Syldavian costumes a get-up? ... Your own national dress?

Syldavian national dress? That?... This is no laughing matter... You know as well as I do those are Greek costumes.

Greek costumes?... But we certainly asked the costumier for Syldavian ones...
I told you he didn't seem very bright.

Anyway, that is quite unimportant... What chiefly interests me is why you were parachuted here...
Us... parachuted? ... We weren't parachuted!

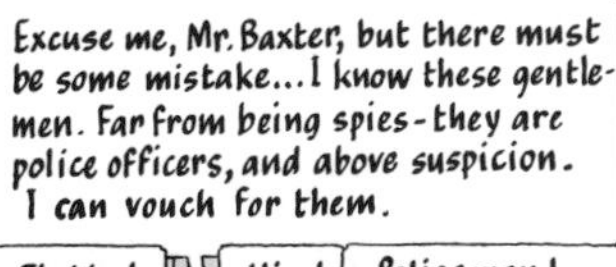
Excuse me, Mr. Baxter, but there must be some mistake... I know these gentlemen. Far from being spies - they are police officers, and above suspicion. I can vouch for them.

Tintin!
Him!
Policemen! Them?...

Yes, us!... On a special mission. Our goverment sent us to protect our countrymen.
So it was you I was told about. But in that case you should have some papers...

Papers?... Yes, of course we had papers. But they were stolen on the train!
You can believe them, Mr. Baxter. I'm sure they're telling the truth.

Hello, Control! ... Baxter here ... The two men you arrested are not the parachutists ... Continue the search.

You're free now, gentlemen. Please excuse our mistake.

It's nothing. Just one of the risks of our job!

Now to get back to X-FLR 6. I'd like to say a few words... The trial rocket will soon be ready. I'm sure that's where the spies will concentrate their efforts. So please be especially alert...

If it were possible, Mr. Baxter, I'd very much like permission to leave the Centre for a few days - to make a trip into the mountains. I feel I'd like to stretch my legs.
But of course!... I quite understand your wanting to have a little relaxation.

A few hours later...

Humping a rucksack on your back, blistering your feet with heavy boots, clambering over piles of rock: that's called relaxation!

Aha!... From here there's an unrestricted view... so now to work!
?

Supposing these mysterious para-chutists had an accomplice within the Centre who wanted to hand over the plans... How would they set about it?... All the en-trances are guard- ed!... All of them?... No ...

You see, Snowy, before we left I spent a long time studying a plan of the Centre. And I found two ventilators no one bothers to guard. They think they're inaccessible... Well, I believe there's a way of get- ting at them ...

Let's see, where's the first one?... There!... Yes, that's it... No, you can't reach that; it's a sheer drop... Where's the other one...

There it is!... Well I think there's a way to approach that one... Come on, Snowy, we'll take a closer look.

So there's our ventilator!

I'm going to look. You guard my rucksack, Snowy - and no noise! Those parachutists can't be far away.

There you go! Acrobatics again! You'll break every bone in your body one day!

It's just as I thought. This must be where the spies contact their inside accomplice ... I ...

?
WOOAH! WOOAH!

A BEAR CUB!
WOOAH! WOOAH!
It must have been attracted by the smell of the honey sandwiches in my rucksack...

Well, if you like them, take one... Enjoy your-self, little greedy-guts!

There he goes, with-out waiting for more! ... And he didn't even say thank you!

That's that, eh, Snowy my boy? Here's a piece for you.

Hey, Snowy, what's the matter?
!!

Steady! Steady! You bunch of gluttons!

Crumbs! Here come the parents! That crowns it!

There! Those are for you! Go and get them!

Quick Snowy! Now's our chance to give them the slip. We'll make our way up there.

Funny sort of lift!

Here we are... The first thing is to warn the Captain.
The first thing is to let me down!

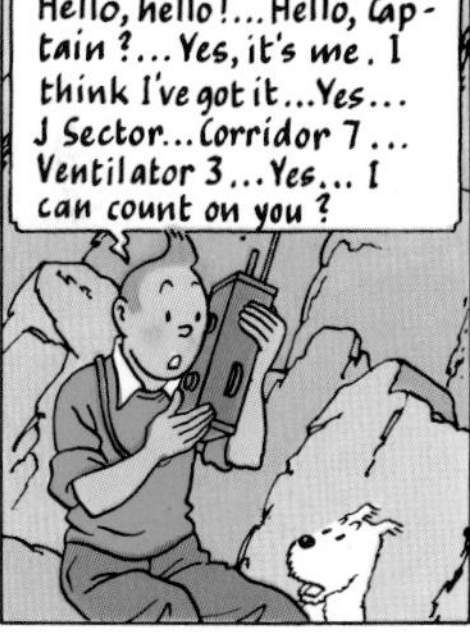
Hello, hello!... Hello, Captain?... Yes, it's me. I think I've got it... Yes... J Sector... Corridor 7... Ventilator 3... Yes... I can count on you?

Trust me!... You said J Sector, Corridor 7, Ventilator 3... Right! No, no, not a word to a soul!

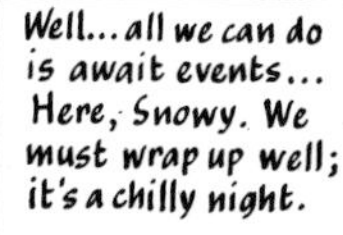

Well... all we can do is await events... Here, Snowy. We must wrap up well; it's a chilly night.

Some hours later...

What's that?... I heard a noise!

That's one of the parachutists! ... But where's the other?

He's approaching the grating... Someone's handing him papers... Now's my moment to join in!

Hands up!
?

Well done, Jim!
BANG

At that moment, inside the Centre...
That's a shot!
From outside! ... I... Hey, I've got someone!... Oh, I've lost him!

Wooa-aa-aa-aah ...
Got him again! ... Quick, help me hold him!
Where are you? ... Ah, there!
Let me go! Here, let me go!... It's me, Frank Wolff!

Ah, the lights have gone on again... Why it's Mr. Wolff!
That's what I tried to tell you!... Meanwhile he's got away...

?
OH!
Great Scotland Yard! Who's that?

The Captain! He's been knocked out!

Now then, what's the meaning of all this hullabaloo?
Mr. Baxter!

That's Snowy howling, Mr. Baxter. Something must have happened to Tintin. Hurry! He's out there, near the ventilator grid.

Hello, Control?... Baxter here... Send a search party at once to look for Tintin... Outside... J Sector... Corridor 7... Ventilator 3... Hurry!... Keep me informed at Post 18.

Now Captain, tell me what happened to you.

It's like this... Tintin went off this morning, saying he was going to try to catch the parachutists... About five o'clock he called me by radio: he was convinced he'd found the place where the intruders...

... would try to contact their accomplices. According to him it was the ventilator grid in this corridor. Events proved him right!... In the evening I lay in wait here... It was well on into the night when the lights suddenly went out, leaving the corridor in total darkness. I heard a rustling beside me, and that moment I thought my head had burst!
And you, Wolff?

Well, I happened to see the Captain as he left his quarters... There was something ... er... odd about him and it intrigued me... I followed him. When he hid, I did the same... Time passed... Then, as he said, the current went off. I heard a dull thud, and the sound of a body falling... I leapt forward... There was a shot outside... then shouts... Someone jostled me in the dark... And then I found myself in the hands of these men.
Very odd...

And what are you doing here at this hour gentlemen?
In all sincerity Director-General, I can solemly and truthfully say...

BHOPP
BHOPP

Forgive us... It's some extraordinary pills we once took... in Arabia[1]... Their effect recurs sometimes.

RRRRING
Oh! The telephone...

Hello!... Yes... You've found him? He's hurt?... What did he say?... Oh, he's unconscious... In the sick-bay?... You're waiting for the doctor?... All right. I'm coming at once.

[1] See Tintin in the Land of Black Gold

If we may, Mr. Baxter, we'll stay here... We might pick up some clues.
You think so?... All right.

I don't know why, but it strikes me that Baxter and Wolff are behaving suspiciously.
To be precise: most auspiciously

We'll take care of them later. Meanwhile, let's have a look at this famous ventilator...

I don't see anything special..

I say, look!

That door: it's ajar... Perhaps that's where...
You're right: let's see.

Wait, I'll switch on the light.

!
!

What's all this paraphernalia?

?

You stay here... I'm going to see what's behind that door.
Right!

?

EEEEEEEK!
!

What's the matter?...You're white as a sheet!... Here, tell me. And stop your teeth chattering!... Now, what is it?

A sss... a sss... a skeleton! ... I saw a skeleton!...There, behind that screen!
A skeleton? My poor friend, you're talking through your hat!

I... I assure you...
Now then, don't be silly. You come with me!

There... you see? Where's your skeleton now, eh?

But I'm quite sure...
You are?... Oh well, if you see it again, give it my love!

A skeleton!... Ha! ha! ha! Poor old Thomson, he's off his rocker!...

Oh, my stick!

EEEEEEEEK!

The sss... the sss... the skeleton!... You were right!... I saw it too... There... behind that screen again!
You too!... Now you see I wasn't dreaming!

Now keep calm!... No one leave the room!... And don't picnic... I mean panic... We'll proceed with caution... and look around...
That's... that's it... We'll look around...

Nothing... That's queer...
Where the devil can it have gone?
X-RAY

Keep your eyes open!... It can't have gone far.
12

In here, perhaps?

Hey, psst!... Quick, Thompson, come and look!
?

?

W-w-we must act at... at... at once! At once! T-t-take him b-b-b-by surprise! ... Now, keep calm!... Get your gun out: he may be armed.
All... all... all... all right!

Hands... hands... hands... hands up!

Hands up, I said! Oh, so you won't! ... Well, in that case I'll... I'll... I'll...

Very well... But make one false move and I'll shoot! Understand?... Put the handcuffs on him, Thomson.
?

Now, get going!... Quick march!... You don't want to?... Passive resistance, eh?... Grab him, Thomson!
!

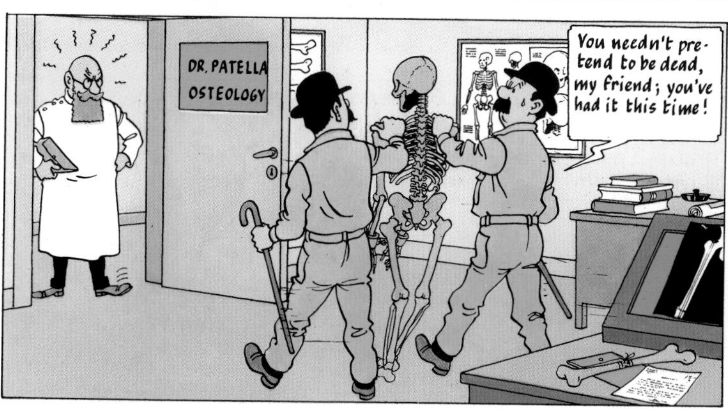
DR. PATELLA
OSTEOLOGY
You needn't pretend to be dead, my friend; you've had it this time!

Meanwhile...
Calling KM 2... Calling KM 2... First mission completed... First mission completed...
O.K.! We'll have their rocket, now!

Meanwhile . . .
No, luckily it's nothing serious. The bullet only grazed the skull... Of course, it was a violent blow. But he's come round completely now, and you can question him.

...Then I leapt forward and shouted "Hands up!"... He obeyed... At that moment I heard an explosion, and instantly I felt a terrific crack on my head... It was the other parachutist, whom I hadn't seen. To save his accomplice he fired at me.

The gangsters!... The pirates! ... If I get my hands on those crooks, I'll tear them apart like... like... like...

CRACK

I... Forgive me, Mr. Baxter... I'm terribly sorry... Wait... I'll get you another chair.

No need, thank you!... Where were we?... Oh yes... The next thing is to find out which documents are missing. And above all, we must unmask the traitor in our midst, spying on all our activities.

I'm afraid that won't be easy. Now the fellow has achieved his object he will try to be inconspicuous. As for our discovering which documents he gave to his accomplices. I'm certain he won't have been foolish enough to steal the originals, and so help us to narrow our search.

To my mind he would simply have made copies. If I hadn't been there tonight the spy would have handed over his stuff to his accomplice, quite quietly, with no one any the wiser.

You're right!.. But still, we'll continue our inquiry. Meanwhile I'll ask Calculus to speed up preparations for launching the trial rocket... With that I'll leave you... Get well soon.

Are you coming, Captain?
If I may, I'll stay with Tintin.

Look Captain, it's late and...
None of that!... I'm staying here!... A full pipe and a comfortable chair, that's all I ask...

!
?

Some weeks later. The day for the launching of the trial rocket has arrived.
Well, Professor?
Everything is ready, Mr. Baxter. The last guide rails are in place ... The gantries have been removed. The technicians are now...

... completing the fuelling - up.

Hello, Mr. Baxter... Look who's here...
See! They've almost finished.

Tintin! You?... I thought you were still confined to your room.
I am, in theory! But I wouldn't miss the launching of the trial rocket for anything.
Look, Mr. Baxter. Tintin's better!

Finished!

Finished!... Everything's ready. I'll clear the bay.
Good idea... But don't forget to clear the bay!

Oh! I'm sorry!
Wooah!

All very well to apologise! Why doesn't he look where he's going!

At any rate, I'll be safe up here!

Ah, peace at last!

Attention please!... Clear the launching bay... Attention please!... Clear the bay...

?
I repeat ...
All right! I heard!

Clear the launching bay!

All out ?... Splendid !... We can go to the Control Room.

This is it... From here we shall control the rocket during its flight.
I say, Professor...

... Did you remember the gadget I mentioned to you when you came to see me in the sick-bay ?
The gadget ?... Oh, yes, it's done. I fixed it this evening...

Hello ? Observatory ? ... Is that you, Michael ?... Baxter here. I'm in the Control Room. All ready ?

Absolutely ready, Mr. Baxter... Everybody standing by.

Yes, Radar here... Yes, Mr. Baxter, we're all ready...

Well, now we can only wait for zero hour ... Another twenty minutes.

Why, what's this little device, Professor ? It wasn't here last night !
I ... yes... I put it there... It's an idea of Tintin's.
Oh, just a small detail...

Meanwhile...
All the same it was fishy about that skeleton...

Look what I can see !
Well ? It's a high-tension switch-room.

It may look like a power switch-room. But supposing it isn't, eh ? We'll investigate. Here's my master key.

All the same, be careful.

I'm not a child, am I ? ... Anyway, I...

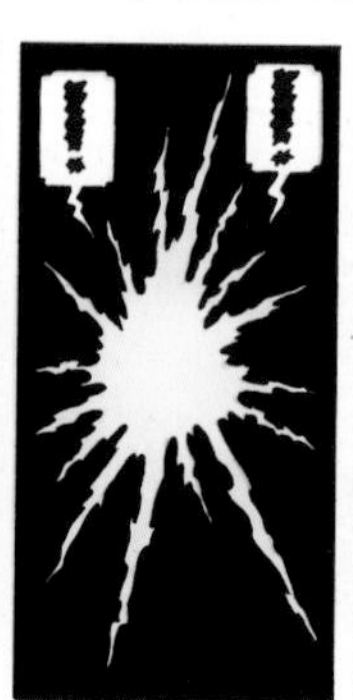

This is the control panel with all the instruments for guiding the rocket.
Aha! It looks a bit like a piano to me!

And here is the celebrated vocalist, Bianca Castafiore of La Scala, Milan, to sing you the famous jewel song from "Faust". "Ah, ♫ my beauty ♪ past compare: these jewels ♫ bright I wear"

AH THESE JEWELS
Sh! Quiet!... Isn't that the alarm siren?
?

And now the great virtuoso Haddocksikoff... Pom ♪ Pom ♪ Pom ♪ Pompity ♫ Pom ♪

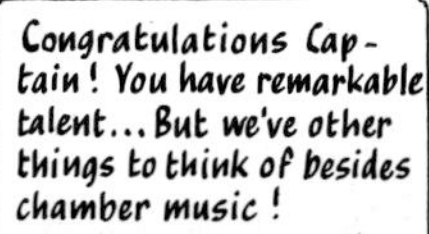
Congratulations Captain! You have remarkable talent... But we've other things to think of besides chamber music!

?

In a few minutes, gentlemen, X-FLR 6 will begin its flight... I propose that the honour of launching the rocket should fall to our youngest colleague - Tintin ... You agree?

The left-hand lever controls the auxiliary engine-used only at the outset. The other controls the nuclear motor which takes over later.

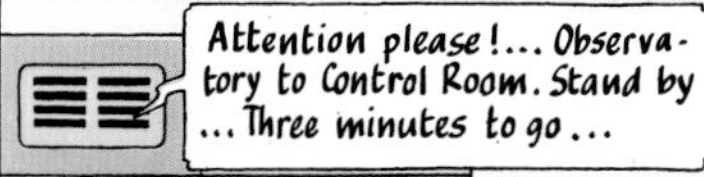
Attention please!... Observatory to Control Room. Stand by ... Three minutes to go...

Action stations!

Two minutes to go...

One minute to go...

Thirty seconds to go...

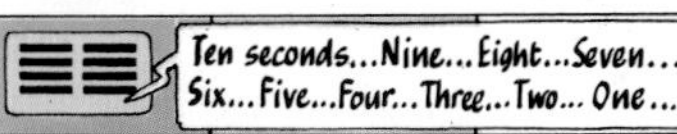
Ten seconds...Nine...Eight...Seven... Six...Five...Four...Three...Two... One...

NOW!
ZERO!

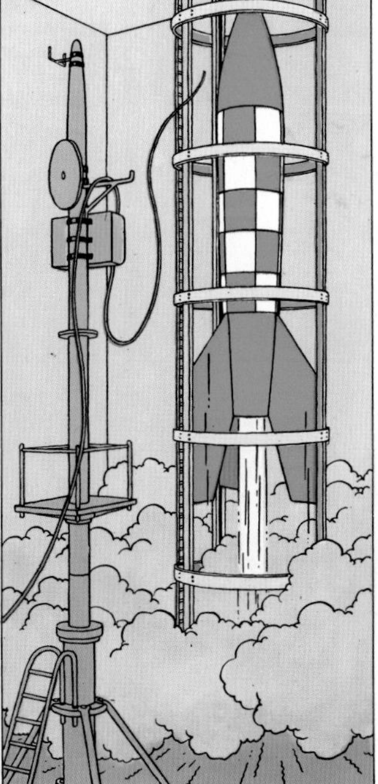

There she goes! For the first time in history man is sending a rocket to the Moon and back!

The Moon and back!... Do you realise what those little words mean: THE MOON AND BACK!
!

Oh dear, I'm so sorry! ... But how lucky your pipe wasn't in your mouth!

Observatory to Control Room ... Stand by to engage nuclear motor ... Ready!... Thirty seconds from now ...

Twenty seconds to go...
Blistering barnacles, where's my pipe?

Ten seconds to go... Nine ... Eight... Seven...
Have you seen my pipe anywhere?
I'm sorry, not now...

Six...Five... Four...three...two ...

One!... ZERO!

Observatory to Control Room... The nuclear motor has just taken over... All going well. Cut the auxiliary engine.

Have you seen my pipe?
?
?

Your pipe? What would I want with your pipe? ... I'm sorry but I haven't time to worry about your pipe now!

Observatory to Control Room... How's the radar working?
Perfectly! All going well!

Meanwhile, many thousands of miles away...
Patience! We can't intervene for some hours yet...

Observatory to Control Room... Correction zero...zero...eight... six... Please repeat.
Zero...zero... eight...six... Correction made...

A trifling correction, I think. But I'd better just check with my tables...

OH!
?

Goodness gracious, Captain! It's you!

Mind out or you'll bump your head!
BONK

Have you lost something?
Have I lost something?... What do you think I'm doing down here?... Picking four-leaf clover?

That goat Calculus! Where did he knock my pipe to?
?

Quiet Snowy!... Be quiet!...
Wooah! Wooah!

Blistering barnacles, will you be quiet!
Wooah! Wooah!

Captain, do please be sensible... Stop teasing the dog.
Me?... Me teasing him?

It's not me... It's him...
Wooah!

YEOW!
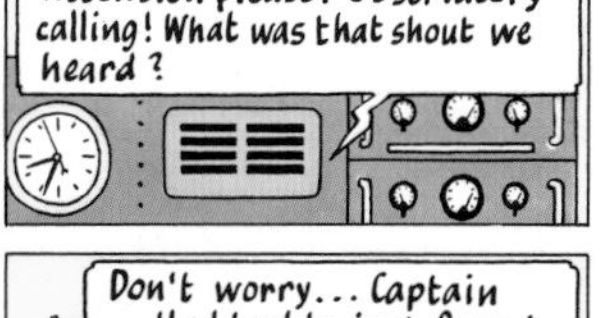
Attention please! Observatory calling! What was that shout we heard?

Don't worry... Captain Haddock's just found his pipe.

Many hours later...
Observatory to Control Room... In three minutes the rocket will enter its orbit round the Moon... Stand by ...

When this phase of the operation begins, the motor is stopped. Its own speed, combined with the force of lunar attraction, should cause the rocket to go round the Moon. We only resume radio-control when X-FLR 6 reappears.

Attention please! In thirty seconds cut the nuclear motor!.. Ready!... Ten seconds to go... Nine... Eight... Seven... Six... Five... Four...

Three... Two... One... ZERO!
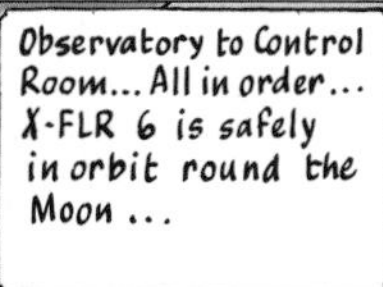
Observatory to Control Room... All in order... X-FLR 6 is safely in orbit round the Moon...

In thirty seconds she will be out of our sight.

There... We can't see her any more.

Meanwhile...
Now their rocket is masked by the Moon!... We go into action in a few minutes...

Just imagine! For the first time in history, cameras are now photographing the side of the Moon no one has ever seen! And it's thanks to us, my dear Wolff! Thanks to us!
Observatory to Control Room ... In three minutes the rocket will reappear ... Stand by to resume radio-control ...

THERE SHE IS!
Yes indeed, there she is!

Observatory to Control Room ... Stand by ... Restart the nuclear motor in thirty seconds ...
D'you think I could do it?
Of course.

Observatory to Control Room ... Ten seconds to go ... Nine ... Eight ... Seven ... Six ... Five ... Four ... Three ... Two ... One ... ZERO!
NOW!
Careful! Not so hard!

The wonders of modern science! ... Just an ordinary lever, and click! ... Hundreds of thousands of miles away an engine starts up! ... It's fantas-tic!
Observatory to Control Room ... Correction: zero, zero, nine, eight ... Repeat ...
Zero, zero, nine, eight. Correction made.

Observatory to Control Room ... Correction: three, two, seven, six ... Repeat ...
Three, two, seven, six ... Correction made.

For heaven's sake make those corrections! You're taking no notice of the figures we're giving!

I beg your pardon, but I've followed you exactly! ... I'm not deaf, am I?

Is something wrong, Wolff?
The rocket is going off course. I don't know what it is ...

Correction: seven, eight, five, two. Correct it, this time!
That's what I'm doing, confound it!

Thundering typhoons, you wretched rocket! Will you get back on your course! You wait! I'll get you!

I can't understand it. The rocket is right out of control!
But surely that's impossible!

I've got it! Tintin was right! ... How lucky I listened to him!
What do you mean?
?

Hi, Professor! Mind your headphones!

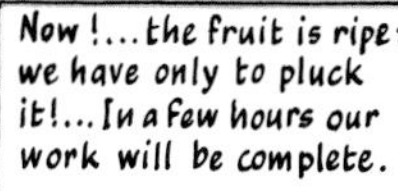
Now!... the fruit is ripe: we have only to pluck it!... In a few hours our work will be complete.

Well done!

What are you doing, Professor?
No, Mr. Baxter, I'm not mad! ... But I don't want our rocket, with all its secrets, to fall into the hands of a Foreign power.
For that's what is happening!... Why won't X-FLR6 obey us? Because it has been intercepted by a stronger radio-control station than ours, on the same wave-length!... If we don't intervene, there's no knowing who may lay hands on our rocket!

As sure as my name's Cuthbert Calculus, that's not going to happen. There is a way: Tintin suggested it. A device to destroy the rocket in flight-and I installed it last night. Mr. Baxter, we must blow up X-FLR6!
Surely you can't mean that?

Observatory to Control Room... The rocket is completely beyond our radio control.
You hear that Mr. Baxter. What do you say?
All right!
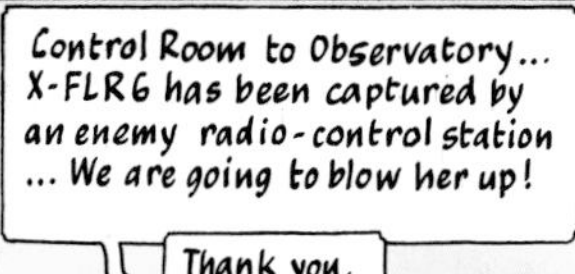
Control Room to Observatory... X-FLR6 has been captured by an enemy radio-control station ... We are going to blow her up!

Thank you, Mr. Baxter.

Be brave, Cuthbert!... Now you must destroy your whole life's work!... There!

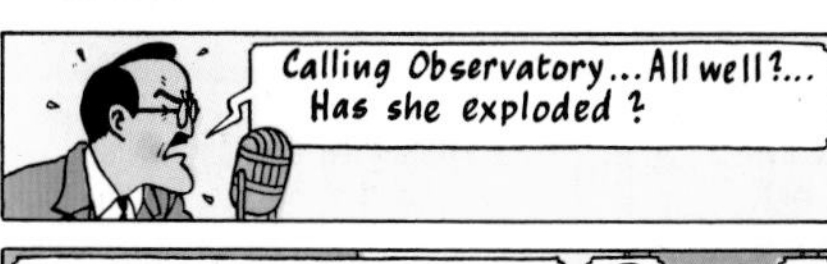
Calling Observatory... All well?... Has she exploded?

Exploded?... No!... On the contrary, she's getting further and further away.
?
!
?

Oh misery!... Misery!... All is lost!... Our secrets, our discoveries, lost!... Everything will drop into foreign hands!... This is appalling!
Here, calm yourself, Professor!... Cuthbert, I implore you!

And the photographs!... The first photographs of the other side of the Moon!... All lost! ... Oh, this is disaster!
OW!

Ah, I see what it is! Two wires disconnected... That can soon be put right.

This time I think it will work ... There!
So sorry!... I thought I was tearing MY hair!

Observatory to Control Room ... X-FLR6 has exploded. There's nothing more to see.

Accursed luck! They've foreseen everything! They'd sooner blow up their rocket than let it fall into our hands!

How did I get the idea?... Well, it occurred to me that the documents passed to the spies might contain all the details of the radio-control of our trial rocket... I confided my fears to Professor Calculus who immediately devised the mechanism to explode X-FLR6, should she be intercepted... You see what a good idea it was.

Too true!... All too true!... All our hopes brought to nothing ... Months, years of research and struggle! All annihilated in a flash!
Look out for my beard! Your grief's a bit wild...

No, Professor Calculus, all is not lost! On the contrary, this is a triumph for you... Didn't your nuclear motor work perfectly? Didn't the rocket go to the Moon, and circle it?

Tintin is right! The trial was conclusive. Don't be so downhearted. Tomorrow we start work on another rocket. But not an experimental one - this will be the real Rocket, to carry you to the Moon!

To the Moon!... Hooray!

A fortnight later...
I'm fed up with hanging about here, doing nothing.

I ought to have stayed peacefully at Marlinspike, instead of fooling about in this dump, just to gratify the whims of a mad professor!

There he goes now ... I'll tell him a thing or two!... Hi, Professor!

Look here, I've had enough of going round in circles in this confounded Centre! How soon do you propose this little week-end trip to the Moon?
Really?... You too?... Do you?

That's very odd. I have the same thing myself. But mine's in the right shoulder... A touch of rheumatism, I expect,.. It has been damp these last few days. But it will go. Excuse me: Mr. Baxter is waiting...

Good morning, Mr. Baxter.
Good morning, Professor. You've brought the blueprint of the rocket?

I'm afraid not, Mr. Baxter. But the blueprint is finished... Here... What do you think of it?

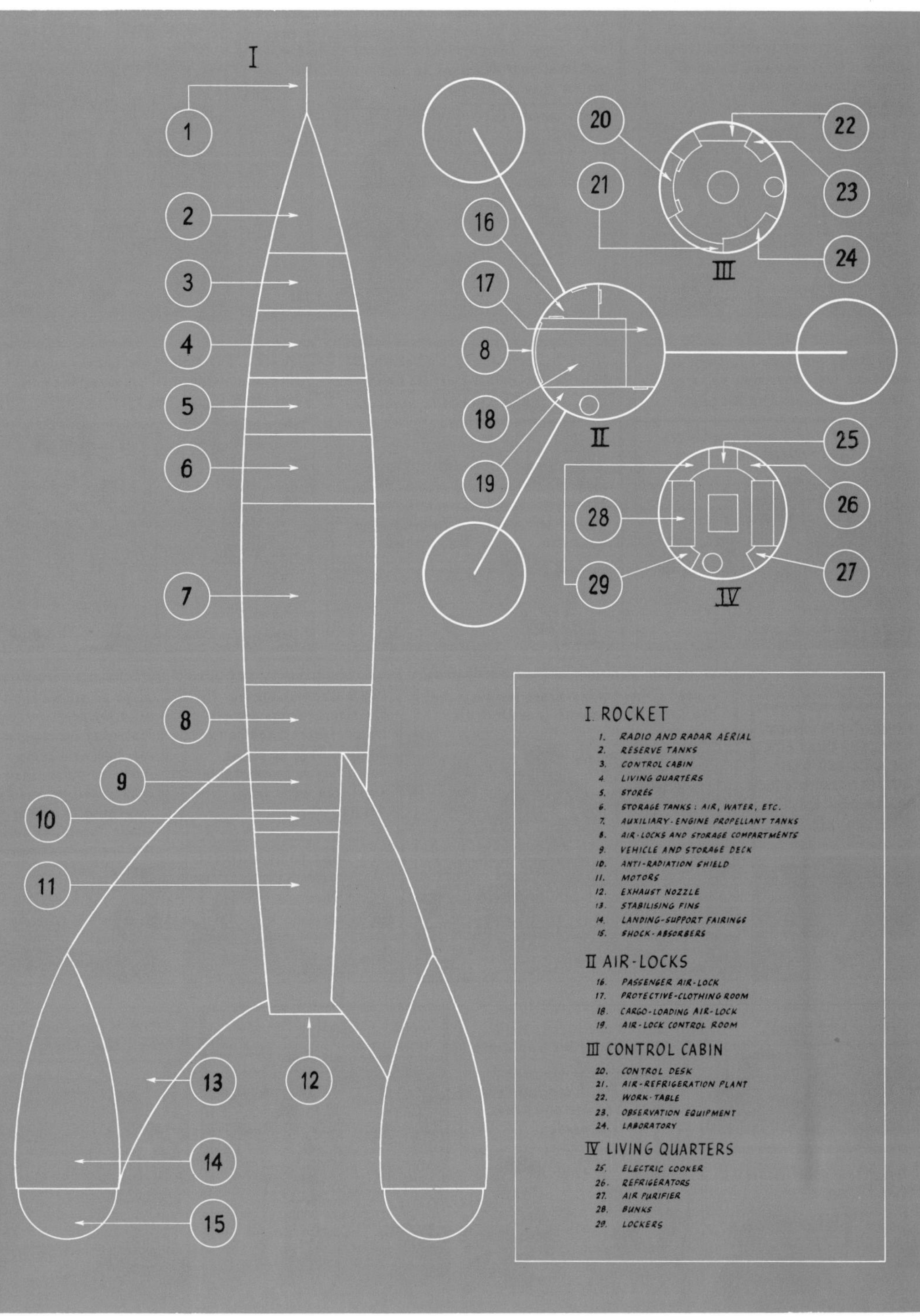
I. ROCKET
1. RADIO AND RADAR AERIAL
2. RESERVE TANKS
3. CONTROL CABIN
4. LIVING QUARTERS
5. STORES
6. STORAGE TANKS: AIR, WATER, ETC.
7. AUXILIARY-ENGINE PROPELLANT TANKS
8. AIR-LOCKS AND STORAGE COMPARTMENTS
9. VEHICLE AND STORAGE DECK
10. ANTI-RADIATION SHIELD
11. MOTORS
12. EXHAUST NOZZLE
13. STABILISING FINS
14. LANDING-SUPPORT FAIRINGS
15. SHOCK-ABSORBERS
II AIR-LOCKS
16. PASSENGER AIR-LOCK
17. PROTECTIVE-CLOTHING ROOM
18. CARGO-LOADING AIR-LOCK
19. AIR-LOCK CONTROL ROOM
III CONTROL CABIN
20. CONTROL DESK
21. AIR-REFRIGERATION PLANT
22. WORK-TABLE
23. OBSERVATION EQUIPMENT
24. LABORATORY
IV LIVING QUARTERS
25. ELECTRIC COOKER
26. REFRIGERATORS
27. AIR PURIFIER
28. BUNKS
29. LOCKERS

Splendid, Professor! My heartiest congratulations! To me this looks admirable, from every point of view. When do you plan to start construction?
Tomorrow, if you agree.

Right!... I'll go and give the necessary instructions. The services of every skilled man will be at your disposal at once. Work will go on day and night.
That's wonderful. Thank you!

Here he comes again!
Goodbye, Mr. Baxter.

Look here, you didn't answer my question just now. How soon is your little trip to the Moon?
Well, if I were you I'd try camphorated oil.
BAXTER

Blistering barnacles, it's nothing to do with camphorated oil! It's the Moon..
Rubbed in night and morning.

You nitwit you! I'm talking about your trip to the Moon!

Maybe... But believe me, there's nothing like camphorated oil... Excuse me now. I'm up to my eyes in work.

Some months later..
Hello... Yes Mr. Baxter, we're going ahead with the space-suit trials... Captain Haddock is our guinea-pig... Yes, I'll keep you informed.

I say!... Your fancy-dress weighs a ton! You can't move a muscle with it on.

Don't worry, Captain. On the Moon things are six times lighter than on the Earth... Once up there, you'll feel as comfortable as if you were in a lounge suit.
Glad to hear it!

First of all we'll reduce the pressure. Yesterday we completed air-tightness tests with the suits. They were excellent... If anything is wrong, shout "Stop" and we'll restore normal pressure at once.

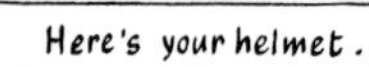
Here's your helmet.

I feel like a goldfish in its bowl!

Testing the radio... Hello... Can you hear me, Captain?
Yes, I can hear you. You can start now, I'm ready.

Good!... Goodbye for now. Good luck!
Thanks.

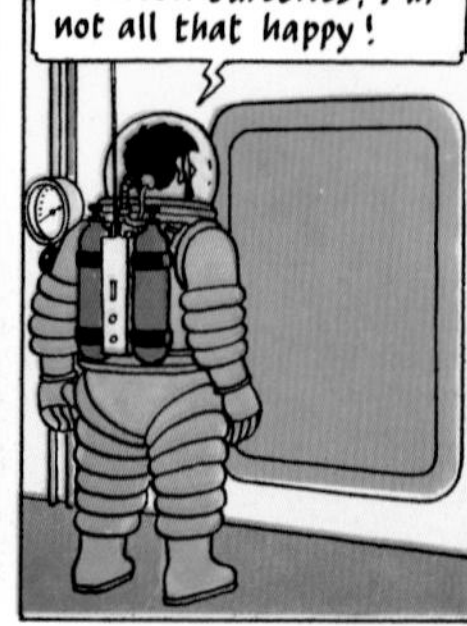
Between ourselves, I'm not all that happy!

Hello Captain!... Ready?
Carry on!

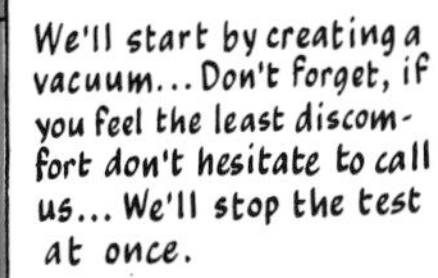
We'll start by creating a vacuum... Don't forget, if you feel the least discomfort don't hesitate to call us... We'll stop the test at once.

O.K.

50
25
0
100

Pressure is now down to zero... You are almost in an absolute vacuum... How are you feeling?
Not bad, thanks. And you?

Now... We are going to lower your temperature. Don't forget to adjust your heating apparatus.
Right...

Brrr... It's certainly starting to get beastly cold...

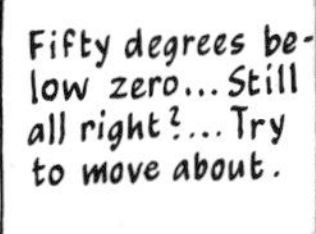
Fifty degrees below zero... Still all right?... Try to move about.

Try to move about? With all this paraphernalia on? I'd like to see you do it. I suppose you could walk on your hands!

?

Hello Captain... That's fine!... Carry on!

Excellent... Now you can see...

...that it's not so difficult after all!

All right Captain, you can stop.

Hello Captain, what are you doing?... Hello!

For heaven's sake Mr. Wolff, bring the pressure and temperature back to normal at once! Something's wrong!
?

All right if I open it now ?
Carry on !

Great snakes!

Keep still ! I'll take off your hel-met.

?
?
?

Mice! Snowy ! Here, Snowy !
Wooah ! Wooah !

Good gracious ! They're the mice we used for the first tests! We forgot to take them out of the suit !

But why didn't you call out ? I told you...
Blistering barnacles, that's what I did. It was you... You didn't answer !

You could have called for ever, Captain. Your radio equipment is disconnected !
Disconnected! It'll be fun if that happens on the Moon!

Anyway, it has proved that the suit is ab-solutely resistant to a vacuum, and low temperatures... What happened was just a little incident... quite unimportant ...

HELP ! ... HELP !
What, Captain ?
?
?

That's the Thomsons! Hurry, we must see...

M-m-m... m-mice!... It's alive with mice in here!

Now what's happened to that pair of sea-gherkins?

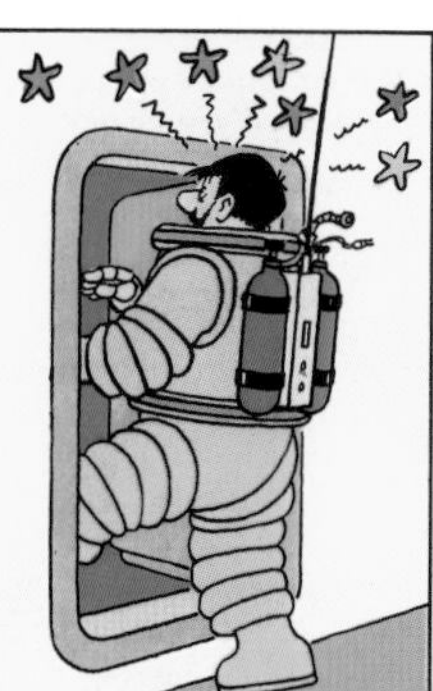

My poor friend! Didn't you notice the door was rather low?

D'you think I did it on purpose?... I suppose you think my favourite pastime is cracking my head against doors? Well, I've had enough! I've had enough of being a playmate for neurotic mice!

I've had enough, d'you understand?... You want to go to the Moon?... Well go! But without me! I'm going home to Marlinspike!... And you can go on acting the goat here for as long as you like!

Oh, I'm acting the goat? ... I'm acting the goat, am I?... I... This... this is too much! I, acting the goat!... I demand an apology... An apology, you hear? ... You have no right to say such a thing!... Acting the goat!

To dare say such a thing to me!... You!... You!... You follow me... I'll show you just how I act the goat!... Come along!

Oho! I'm acting the goat!
Look, I... I...

So, I act the goat?
I didn't mean anything...

You see, I was feeling upset... just then... But it's all over now.

PIONNNG

Billions of blue blistering barnacles! If ever I find the pirate who did that I'll make him dance, I promise you!

It was your aerial, Captain... You...

So you're trying to give me the slip? Well, you aren't going to! Come on! Hurry!

So I act the goat!

Slaving for two months non-stop, working myself to the bone, all to hear myself called a goat!... It's too much!

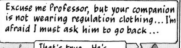

Excuse me Professor, but your companion is not wearing regulation clothing... I'm afraid I must ask him to go back...
That's true... He's right... I ought to...

Begone, you worm! Out of my sight! I'm acting the goat, d'you hear?

Professor, I implore you...
I'm acting the goat, eh?

And I suppose these people are acting the goat, eh?

Yes, this is the Chief of Internal Security... What?... Professor Calculus?... Making a scene? Says he's acting the goat?... I'll teach him to act the goat...

And the atomic pile, never stopping?... The uranium being made?... The laboratories working day and night?... That's all acting the goat too, I suppose?

Well, Professor, what's all this about? I hear someone's acting the goat.
!

?!
CRRR
GRRR
KRRRR

For heaven's sake, Cuthbert, calm yourself!

For months, teams of experts have been worked to death... acting the goat, of course!

Come on!...Sit down there and don't argue ... We're leaving!
But...

Good morning, Professor. Will you sign the dispatch book, please?
For the love of heaven don't let him go!

Stand aside, microbe!... Let me pass! I'm acting the goat, d'you hear?... I'm acting the goat!
252

Stop them!... They've no exit permit!

Hello!... Garage here...A jeep driven by Professor Calculus has left without permission ...Stop it!

Quick, clear the entrance and close the doors. There's a jeep coming...

Halt!
Hey!... Stop!
252

Make way for the goat!
?

I often say to myself: one of these days I'll learn to drive! Nowadays everyone should be able to drive a car!

Stop! We're here.

??!
?!
Well, what do you think of that? Look what the goat created.

Well, what about it?... Look what I created – I, Cuthbert Calculus!... And that, I suppose, is what you call "acting the goat"?

You think this... this crackpot contraption will take you to the Moon? ...

This crackpot contraption, as you call it, is taking you to the Moon, as well ... Understand? Meanwhile, you're going to look over it... And put your aerial down!

LIFT!...

Poor Calculus, he must have a screw loose... How do you suppose that monument could go up in the air?... You might just as well play a penny whistle in front of Nelson's Column and expect it to dance a samba!

Not a hope, you know! It wouldn't even stand up by itself!

!
23

You road-hog!... Bully!... Steam-roller!... Cyclotron!

Aren't you ashamed of yourself? Making a scene in front of everybody?... Stand up!... The lift is waiting!

In you go!... Hurry up!
You... you're sure it won't take off without warning?
Meanwhile...

Hello... Hello... yes... I've just had a message from our new agent... The launching takes place in a month: June the 3rd., at 1:34 a.m.... Yes, that's it. Send Colonel Jorgen to me.

First of all, this is the Control Cabin.

Well, what do you think of it ?... You can't call this acting the goat, eh ?
Fantastic !... Er... what are all these bits and pieces for ?

All these bits and pieces, sir, are instruments for navigation and control. On the main instrument desk are the controls for the nuclear motor, the auxiliary engine, radar, wireless, television, automatic air purifier, etc...

To the left of the desk are the oxygen cylinders... That's the periscope, in the middle of the cabin, with its projection screen ...But believe me, you'll have plenty of time to get to know all this equipment.

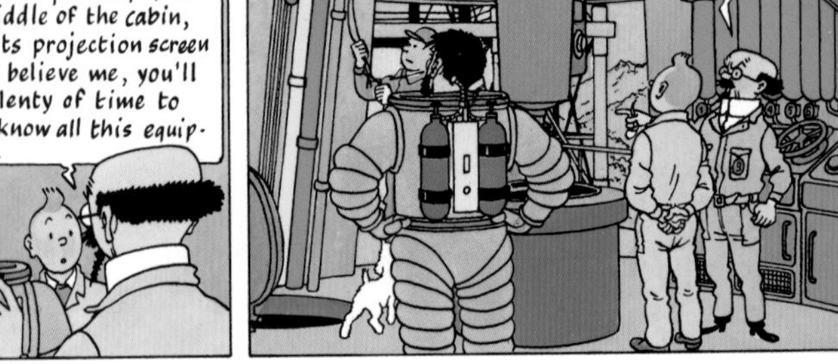
And there's the laboratory, still in the process of construction.

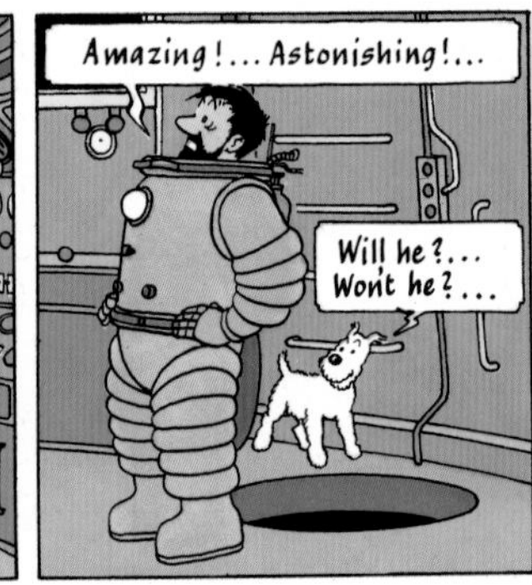
Amazing !... Astonishing !...
Will he ?... Won't he ?...

Take care! Look out, behind you!

I believe you do it on purpose, don't you ?... Every time there's a chance to bump yourself, or sprawl on the floor, you take it !... Can't you pay attention ?

Anyway, you go through this hatch to the deck below. Follow me: I'll lead the way.

And mind out ! There's another hatchway to the left of the ladder...

We are now in the living quarters. This will be our bedroom, kitchen, and dining room, all in one.

And there are the bunks we lie on when...
Blistering barnacles !

Whew! That was near!
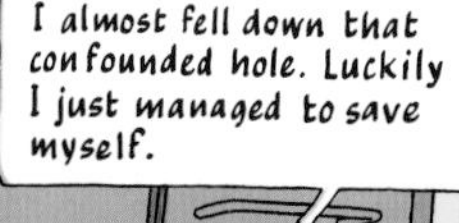
I almost fell down that confounded hole. Luckily I just managed to save myself.

You see?... Even after I told you to be careful!... I know I may act the goat, but at least I look where I am going!... Now we'll go down to the next deck.

As you'll notice, this compartment is deeper than the others: it's twice the depth of a normal one...

Once and for all, Captain, do take care! There's another hatch here. You be careful too, Tintin. And mind Snowy...

There are the storage tanks... Drinking water, and motor propellant. The propellant is for the auxiliary engine, which, as you know, is for launching and landing.

Stars above, Captain! Don't stand so near that hole! Are you trying to break your neck?

To make it possible to leave and re-enter the rocket when we are in space, we've had to provide a system of air-locks... You will see the mechanism for these on the deck below...

I warn you, Captain, there's another hatch... I beg you to take care!

This is the panel controlling the opening of the air-locks...

Attention please!... Professor Calculus to report to the Centre immediately...
Listen!

Right, I'll go... You can look round the large storage compartment, through that door... I'll come straight back.

And look where you're going, Captain... There's a step!

?
!

Good heavens! Poor Professor Calculus!... No bones broken, I hope.

Blistering barnacles! What's happened?
Here are your glasses... Are you all right?

Before you start preaching at others to be careful, you'd do better to watch your own feet, sea-gherkin! You're lucky to be still in one piece!

Who... who are you? And what's that fancy dress?

Fancy dress?... Look here, don't begin acting the... er... I mean, don't try pulling my leg! We've had enough of that! ...

Ah, I've found you at last, Professor.

This is a fine thing! What a way to behave... and you a responsible man... It's preposterous!... You nearly caused a dozen accidents! ...What's biting you?

I... er... I don't understand ...What...what do you want? ... Where am I?
?
?

Where are you?... Billions of blue blistering barnacles, you know as well as we do where you are, you anacoluthon!

Look, Professor, you remember!... You were just showing us over your Moon-rocket... Professor?... Professor?

I think this is serious ... I believe he's lost his memory... We must take him back to the Centre without delay, and warn Mr. Baxter at once.

Calculus?... Amnesia?
I'm afraid so... The doctors are examining him now.

Well, gentlemen, it's not too bad is it?... You'll cure him for us?
Hmm!
Umm!

Hmm, it's hard to say...One can't tell at once... We must wait and see...There may be some improvement... One should never give up hope...
At all events, it's a most interesting case.

But he *must* be cured! He alone, he alone, d'you hear, knows the secret of the nuclear motor! Without him the Moon project is impossible ...Impossible, you understand?...
!
!
?
?

Hmm... yes... I see... Well, we'll do all we can... But try to amuse him yourselves, to arouse some memory... That sometimes works... It is also possible that a violent shock might bring back his memory.

Some days later...

Marlinspike... Marlinspike Hall... Our butler, Nestor ... Remember Marlin-spike... The Captain ...

That's no good... Let me try... The doctor told us to amuse him... A fortnight ago we had that fancy-dress party at the Centre... You remember the guard on horse-back... Well, you'll see...

Tarantarantaraa... Guards, prepare to attack!...
?

CHAAARGE!

CLIPPETYCLOP CLIPPETYCLOP

Nothing!.. Not a flicker!
Nothing at all!

We must try something else... A violent shock, perhaps?

Look here, Tintin. Let's try this... It's a trick camera I managed to borrow. That'll wake him up!

A pretty picture of our little Cuthbert?... Now then, smile please!... Watch the birdie!

PHHHHHHHHT!

Blistering barnacles, that's no use! He reacted about as much as a tombstone!

We've simply got to wake him up... to get rid of this thundering amnesia... But how?

Amusing him did no good, nor did a shock... Still, this little snake going PHHHT wouldn't scare anybody.

?

There's nothing for it. We must try something else... Wait, I know what'll do the trick.

A violent shock? ...Well, he'll get one!

Calculus! Prepare to die!

Tintin, I think we've done it... I'm sure he's reacting...

!!!

So that's it! Well, this time I'll use strong mea- sures!...

RRRRING
Hello... No, this is Tintin... Hello Mr. Baxter... I'm afraid not. He's just the same... The Captain is still trying...

Blistering barnacles, look out for squalls this time! When this banger goes off under his chair, he'll recover all right!

You don't think it would be better to..?
Leave it to me: you'll see!

Hurry up!... Outside!

Wait!... This is going to be fun!

What's up? That banger's taking its time!

Just my luck!... The fuse must be out.

As I thought! The thundering fuse has gone out!

Look out, Captain! It's still smoking. Be careful!
BANG

The same evening...
So he needs a shock, eh?... Well this time he'll get one, blistering barnacles!

Whoooo!... Whoooo!... Beware, Cuthbert, I am a gho-o-ost!

Ho-ho-ho! Shake in your sho-o-oes! I have come for your soul!

?

Ten thousand thundering typhoons!

Blistering barnacles!... What possessed me to dress myself up as a ghost?

And he just sits there looking at me, the jelly-fish! You couldn't be frightened, could you? You moth-eaten marmot!

I suppose you think I'm enjoying myself, acting the goat!

You won't catch me trying to cure loss of memory again!

A GOAT?...ME!...

A goat!...A goat!... You dare call me a goat! ...This is too much! You're not getting away with that!

An apology! I demand an immediate apology!
Help!... Help!... He's cured!

A few minutes later ...

Oh, Captain, Captain, what a debt we all owe you!... Thanks to you Calculus has recovered!... This is splendid news!
Er... I didn't do much.

Not much?... My dear Captain, without your help, the journey to the Moon would have been impossible... Don't you realise?
Thundering typhoons! I'd forgotten that!

And here is the Professor to thank you himself.
Oh, Captain!... Give me your hand!

They've told me everything: about my loss of memory, and your devoted care... I thank you, Captain, from the bottom of my heart!
I'm... I'm very touched.

I thank you too in the name of Science! You have made possible the journey to the Moon... I shall never forget that!
And neither shall I!

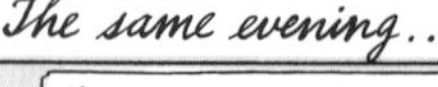
The same evening...

Here's a signal from K.23, sir!
Oh, news from the Main Workshop? Let's hope it is better than last time.

"M.23.301... Mammoth has recovered memory, thanks to Whale." Good old Whale! Without knowing it, he's done us a really good turn... Reply: "M.23.301 received. Operation Ulysses will proceed according to plan."

The days go by...
17
SUNDAY
SATURDAY
15
FRIDAY
THURSDAY
13
WEDNES

... And in one week's time, gentlemen, on the night of the 2nd and 3rd at 1.34 a.m., the launching will take place... Is everything up to schedule?

You, Wolff, are in charge of provisioning and equipment. How are you getting along?

The loading is going ahead. Food supplies, and all the components for our reconnaissance tank are already stowed aboard. I'm just waiting for some optical instruments we need to establish an observatory on the Moon.

Unfortunately the factory at Oberköchen tells me there's been a delay in production. But they've definitely promised delivery of the consignment on the eve of our departure... In that case I...
Excuse me one moment.
RRRING
RRRING

Hello... Yes... What? Inside the Security Area? ...Three?... You're questioning them?... All right. Keep me informed.

You heard that, gentlemen ? The ZEPO have just arrested three people wandering inside the Security Area. Of course they said they wanted to climb Mount Zstophnole, and had lost their way... Whenever they arrest anybody it's the same story ...

You see, despite all the precautions we take, a determined man can always find a way through the defences.

But where were we ?... Oh yes... So on your side, Wolff, everything is in order, except for the delay with the optical instruments... What about you Captain? Air supply, temperature, safety equipment...
All in order !

And you, Professor ?

Everything is ready, Mr. Baxter, except for Snowy's space-suit. That is just being finished now.
?

There we are... Nothing more except to test the radio...

Who's this nice bone for, Snowy?

Golly, what a bone !

Wooah ! ... Wooah !
Fine!... It's working perfectly !

Now, gentlemen, it only remains for me to thank you, and congratulate you. For you have managed to surmount all the obstacles that seemed to stand in the way of making rockets of this type.

Are you coming, Captain ?... We'll go and find Snowy in the laboratory...
Coming ... Coming...

I say... Look at Calculus ... Doesn't anything strike you ?
No... Not at first glance.

It does me ! ... But then I don't walk about with my eyes shut !

Billions of blue blistering barnacles!... And all through looking at our wonder-boy Calculus! Thundering typhoons!

And just why were you looking at the wonder-boy?
?

There, you see?... He isn't deaf any more! He can hear as well as you and me!

Oh, now I understand.

In the first place, I never was deaf... Just a little hard of hearing in one ear... But for the Moon journey I need to hear the radio signals perfectly... So that's why I obtained a hearing aid...

You couldn't have told us before, could you?... And stopped me from bumping into that door! ... And of all the crazy things...
But...
He's right: let's close this door.

... to keep leaving doors open...

Billions of blue blistering barnacles!... Who's the joker who shut this door?... Why couldn't he wait till I'd gone out?...

Thundering typhoons! I forgot to pick up my pipe.

They've left that door open again!

Poor Captain Haddock ... Never any luck!

Billions of blue blistering barnacles!... Did you do that on purpose?
I'm awfully sorry, but how could I know you were coming back?

That's the last time a door wallops me! ... Ah, here's my pipe... Lucky it isn't broken!

Good news, Mr. Baxter!
!

Meanwhile...
Your mind's made up, Colonel?
Absolutely!... Don't forget that I have an old score to settle with our young friend Tintin!

Now then Wolff... What's your news ?
Why, I'd forgotten all about it, Mr. Baxter...

A telegram from the works at Oberköchen: the optical instruments will arrive on Monday morning.
Splendid!... Certainly this is excellent news.

Are you going back to the site ?
Yes, I'm going to supervise the loading of equipment.

Would you mind waiting a few minutes for me ? There's one small package to go in my locker on board...
Of course.

A few moments later...
Here I am... I haven't kept you waiting ?
FRAGILE

Not at all... But tell me: what's in that crate behind you ?
Just two or three bottles of whisky... You know it may be freezing cold up there, so I'm just taking precautions...
I'm awfully sorry, Captain, but no alcoholic liquor is allowed on board... We've a little rum, for emergencies, but that's all... And what's in this parcel ?
Er... A little tobacco for my pipe.

Forgive me, Captain, but I have explicit instructions; no smoking on board... The oxygen supplies are more than sufficient for the journey, there and back, but we can't waste them ... Believe me, I'm terribly sorry ...

So, it's like that, is it?... You don't think I'll go up in your flying cigar under such conditions, do you?... Never, you hear me, never! This is the end: I've had enough. You go to the Moon! Go to Mars, or Jupiter, or dance with the Great Bear if you want!

As for me, my decision is final: I'm not going!
FRAGILE

Hello, Captain... You look cross. Is anything wrong ?

Anything wrong, blistering barnacles? Only that I'm not allowed to take a little whisky and a few ounces of tobacco! And under such conditions I refuse to go!... That's what's wrong!

No "ifs" or "buts" or "maybes"... Once for all, I'm not going!... And don't let me have to tell you again ...

How right you are!
?

Why?... What do you mean?

Well, you're very wise not to go on such a wild goose chase!... It's a ridiculous idea!... Besides, at your age it would be sheer madness!
To be precise: sheer madness at your age.

What? At my age?!... I suppose you take me for a rusty old tub, ready for the scrap-heap?... You'll see how old I am, you Bashi-bazouks!... I'm going, d'you hear?... And I'll send you a postcard from the Moon!

The following Monday... ...
RRRING
RRRING
RRRING

Hello?... Yes... Oh, it's you Wolff ... What is it?..

The optical instruments have arrived safely, Mr. Baxter. They're being stowed aboard now... The launching can take place tonight, at the scheduled time...

Meanwhile...
From these tables you can tell instantly, with the aid of your electronic computers, the exact position and velocity of our rocket...

Good gracious Captain, what an enormous letter!
This is no letter, young man... it's my Will!

And that evening...
Gentlemen, the great day - or rather, the great night - has arrived... In a few hours you will embark upon the greatest adventure the world has ever known... How anxiously we shall follow your progress towards the Moon!

For you will certainly run grave risks... A simple short-circuit means a crash on the Earth or the Moon, or an everlasting journey in space... There are great hazards on landing, and taking off from the Moon... You may be pulverised by meteorites...

You are aware of all these dangers, and you have chosen to brave them... But there is another thing... The fate of the trial rocket could be re-enacted... Our enemies could try to divert you from your course by giving you false directions, in order to seize the rocket...

It looks like being a jolly outing!

Never fear Mr. Baxter... We would all prefer to blow ourselves up, rather than let that happen!

Good-evening, Minister ... This is Miller speaking... I've just received the following signal: "Mission completed. Operation Ulysses going ahead". All is well!

Blow yourselves up? I trust you will not be driven to that extremity! If anything has to go with a bang, let's make it the cork from this bottle! Will you, Captain?

With pleasure, Mr. Baxter... I'm an old hand...

Thundering typhoons! Why does this cork have to be so stubborn?

Would you like me to try, Captain?

Are you proposing to teach me how to open a bottle of champagne?
But...

!
POP

The cork! He's swallowed the cork!

Here, Captain... Sit down... Yes, like that ... Now, I'll give you a thump on the back.

That's better, thanks! But I can't imagine how it happened. It's the first time...

That's got a kick in it!... Champagne doesn't agree with me... It's making my head spin!

Come, gentlemen. The incident is closed... Here, Captain...

Gentlemen, I raise my glass to the success of our enterprise... And I drink the health of the first men to set foot upon the Moon...

And now the hour of departure approaches... The cars are waiting to take us to the launching site... Come, gentlemen!

A few minutes later...
Hail Caesar: those about to die salute thee!... But here they're saluting us, blistering barnacles! And who knows, by thunder: it may be for the last time!...
2537

I must say you don't look very happy, Captain.
Why on earth should I look happy? Because we're off to the Moon?

To the Moon!... Don't make me laugh!... If that honky-tonk Calculus-machine doesn't blow up at the start, we'll find ourselves roaming around between the Great Bear and Jupiter, and never come back! You can hoot with laughter about that if you like!

No, I meant... Oh look, Captain! We're there!

Look! The gantries are floodlit; the rocket is ready for launching! It's like magic!
Yes, very pretty... for the spectators! ...

So there's the machine to which we're entrusting our lives!...It's sheer lunacy!... Just think: through me Calculus recovered his memory, and completed this crazy scheme! I'll never forgive myself!

Meanwhile...
If there's no change of plan, it's just half an hour till their departure...

Gentlemen, the time has come for us to part. As soon as you are inside the rocket, I shall go to one of the shelters to watch the launching. Afterwards, I shall return to the Centre, and resume contact with you by radio.

Goodbye, Captain. I am delighted that a sailor should be one of the first men to set foot on the Moon!
It would have been all the same to me if a piccolo-player had gone!

Goodbye, my young friend. My good wishes go with you! I'm sorry not to be among you...

Look, Mr. Baxter, if you really mean it, I'd be happy to give up my place...
Thank you, Captain, that is most kind. But I would not ask you to make such a sacrifice!

Goodbye, Wolff, and good luck. You know my regard for you... I look to you to stand by the Professor.
Thank you, Mr. Baxter. I shall not fail you.

As for you, my dear Professor - your skill is our best guarantee of success!
Thank you, Mr. Baxter. I can only say this: we will get to the Moon or perish!

Come along. The lift is waiting for us.

Goodness, Captain! You're going to do some reading...
Yes, I want to improve myself...

Would you like some help?
No, thanks. I can manage.

In you go, gentlemen!
Between ourselves, Snowy my boy, I'm in a blue funk!

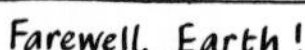

Farewell, Earth!

SLAM

The die is cast!... There they are, inside what could well become their tomb!

Now, I think we'd better run over it again. We all lie down on our bunks. I would remind you...

... that this is the best position during the initial acceleration. Although everything has been done to make this acceleration gradual, it is possible - even probable - that we shall black out. I assure you there's no need to be unduly worried. Naturally one can never tell, but ...

During this first phase of the ascent - I don't know how long it will last - the rocket will be automatically controlled. Afterwards, when we have regained consciousness, we will go up to the control deck and take over for ourselves.

Now, every man to his post for equipment checks.
Tintin, you establish radio contact with Earth.
Right.

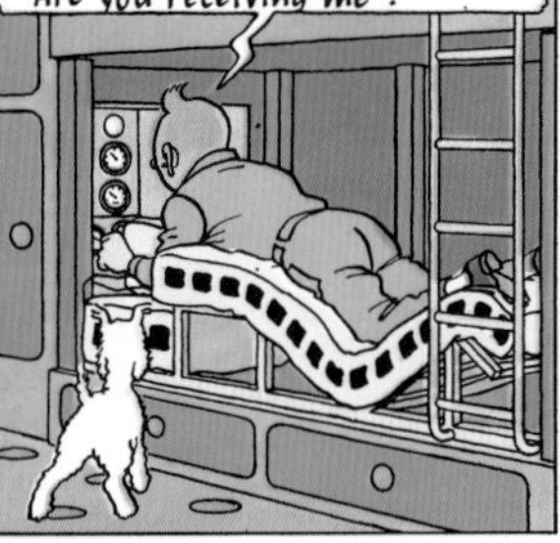
Moon-Rocket calling Earth... Moon-Rocket calling Earth... Are you receiving me?

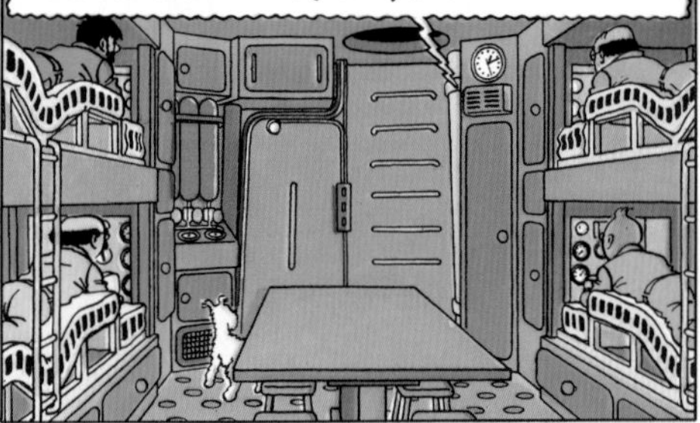
Earth calling Moon-Rocket... Receiving you loud and clear... We are removing the gantries...

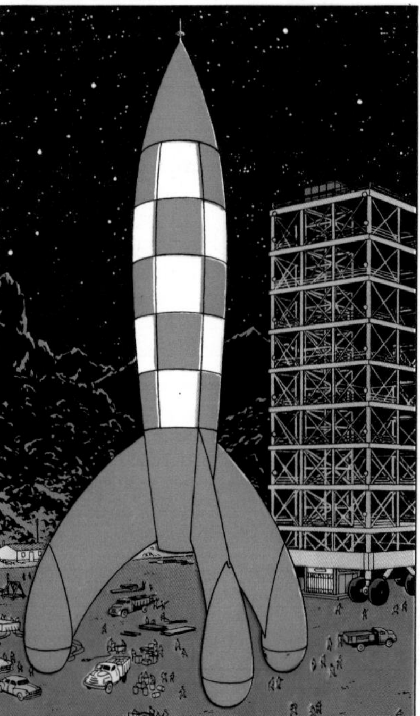

Earth to Moon-Rocket... Gantries removed... We are clearing the launching site...

O. K.

Attention please: clear the launching site!... I repeat: clear the launching site!

Earth to Moon-Rocket... The site is clear... Twenty-eight minutes to go... Are you ready?...

Moon-Rocket ready for launching!

Earth to Moon-Rocket ... You have twelve minutes to go ...

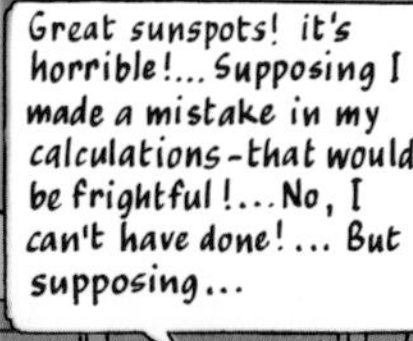
Great sunspots! it's horrible!... Supposing I made a mistake in my calculations - that would be frightful!... No, I can't have done! ... But supposing...

Ten minutes to go ...

Five minutes to go...
Well Tintin old man, you've lived through plenty of adventures... But I wonder if this isn't going to be your last!

Four minutes to go...
Snowy!... Snowy!... Come and lie down, quickly!
Lie down?... Why?... I'm not tired.

Three minutes to go...
What am I doing in this outfit?... And to think I gave that sea-gherkin Calculus his memory back!

Two minutes to go...
What have I done? What have I done?... How could I have let myself get entangled in this dreadful business?

One minute to go...
One minute? Till when?

Will the rocket take off as planned when I press this button, or will everything blow up?

Stand by!... Get ready!... Exactly thirty seconds to go...

Twenty seconds ...
What is that dull steady thumping noise?
THUMP
THUMP
THUMP

It's just the sound of my own heart beating!

Stand by!... Ten seconds...
This is it! There is no turning back... May everything go as we have planned!

Nine... Eight... Seven... Six... Five... Four... Three... Two... One ... ZERO
Into the hands of Fate!

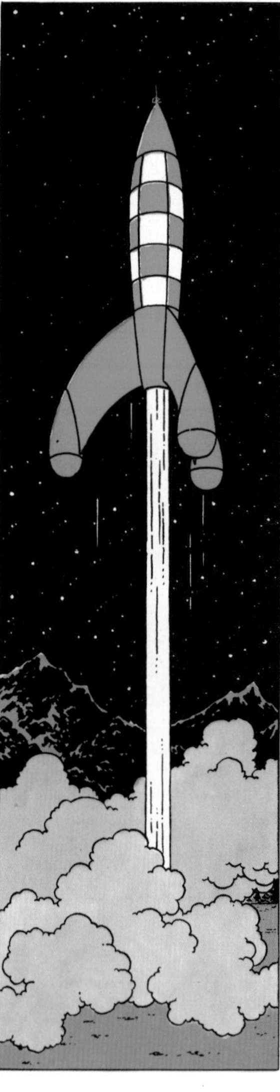

Oooh!... What a horrible crushing sensation!
Blistering barnacles!... It's like having an elephant on my back!

There they go!... They'll probably have blacked out ...Now back to the Control Room...

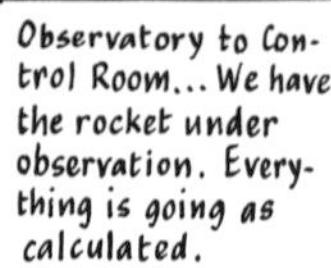
Observatory to Control Room... We have the rocket under observation. Everything is going as calculated.

Observatory to Control Room... The rocket is now 500 miles from the Earth. The nuclear motor has just taken over automatically from the auxiliary engine.
Right. We'll try to make contact with the rocket.

Earth calling Moon-Rocket... Are you receiving me?... Earth calling Moon-Rocket ...Are you receiving me?

Earth calling Moon-Rocket ... Are you receiving me ? ... Are you receiving me ? ...

Observatory to Control Room ... The rocket's altitude is now 1000 miles. Have you succeeded in establishing radio contact yet ? Please report ...

Earth calling Moon-Rocket... Are you receiving me ? ... Earth calling Moon-Rocket...
Control Room to Observatory... The Moon-Rocket is not answering.

Earth calling Moon-Rocket... Are you receiving me ? ... Earth calling...
By Lucifer ! Surely nothing can have gone wrong ?

Ah, Mr. Baxter, you've come back...
Well?

We've been calling them without interruption for some time now... I can't understand it...
Keep on trying.

Earth calling Moon-Rocket ... Are you receiving me? ... Earth calling...
Still no reply... Let's hope...

Observatory to Control Room... The Rocket is now 2,000 miles from the launching point. It has just attained escape velocity, 7 miles per second. Everything seems in order.

Yes, it seems to be so. But what's worrying me is their silence... Call them again, Walter.
Earth calling Moon Rocket...

...Are you receiving me?... Earth calling Moon-Rocket..

What dangers await Tintin and his friends on the Moon?

What will happen on this perilous journey into space?

Will they ever return to Earth? You can join in the rest of their great adventure when you read

EXPLORERS ON THE MOON

HERGÉ

THE ADVENTURES OF TINTIN

EXPLORERS ON THE MOON

EXPLORERS ON THE MOON

The first manned rocket, bound for the Moon, has just been launched from the Sprodj Atomic Research Centre in Syldavia[1]. On board are Tintin, Snowy, Captain Haddock, Professor Calculus, and the engineer Frank Wolff. At the Centre, intense efforts are being made to establish radio contact with the rocket's passengers out in space. Tintin and his friends have fainted from the acceleration on launching. Their recovery is anxiously awaited. The wireless masts stand sentinel in the night sky, but they receive no message . . .
This is Earth calling Moon-Rocket... Are you receiving me?... Earth calling Moon-Rocket...
Suppose we've made a mistake in our calculations!... That would be appalling!
Earth calling Moon-Rocket.. Earth calling...
Meanwhile, unknown to the Centre, others far away are also listening in...
Earth calling Moon-Rocket...
By Lucifer, it's a bad blow for us if they're all dead!

[1] See Destination Moon

Earth calling Moon-Rocket... Are you receiving me?... Earth calling Moon-Rocket...
?

Moon-Rocket, are you receiving me?

WOOAH! WOOAH!
The dog! It's their dog answering!

Tintin!... Tintin!... Wake up!
Ah, he's heard me.

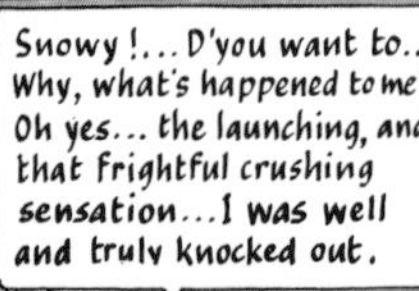
Snowy!... D'you want to... Why, what's happened to me? Oh yes... the launching, and that frightful crushing sensation... I was well and truly knocked out.

Earth calling Moon-Rocket... Are you receiving me?
Earth! It's Earth calling us!
Moon-Rocket calling Earth... This is Tintin here. I've just come round... I'll go and see how the others are.
I'm very well, thanks! But you aren't seriously trying to make me believe we're on the way to the Moon, are you?

Moon-Rocket to Earth... The Captain has just come round... Oh, and there's the Professor recovering....
...and Wolff too... So we're all safe and sound... What is our position please?

Earth to Moon-Rocket ...You are now 2,500 miles from the Earth. Your course is exactly as estimated.

Two thousand five hundred miles from the Earth! Do you realise what an extraordinary adventure this is for us? ...It's unbelievable!...It makes one's head spin!

Well, my head's not spinning, anyway! This whole thing is nothing but hocus-pocus and jiggery-pokery! You're just acting the... I mean... You're trying to pull my leg again!

So you doubt my word, eh? Well, you come up with me.

Golly!... Look over there!
!

Oh, so here you all are. ... Whatever happened? ... An earthquake?

Where in heaven's name have you sprung from?

From the hold. We decided to inspect the rocket before it goes. What's the time?

The time? ... It's two o'clock in the morning!
Good... and the launching is set for 1.34? So we've plenty of time.

Plenty of time!... My poor friends, the rocket left the Earth half an hour ago. We are on our way to the Moon!

Ha! ha! ha! That's a good one! Always ready for a laugh, Professor!
To be precise: Ha! ha! ha!

Earth to Moon-Rocket ... You are now 5,000 miles from the Earth. Your velocity is 6·9 miles per second.

This... this is a joke, isn't it? ... You're just trying to frighten us? The launching really was fixed for 1.34?
1.34 a.m., yes!... Not 1.34 p.m.!

1.34 a.m.?... Not 1.34 p.m.? ... Great Scotland Yard! We thought it was 1.34 in the afternoon!

Moon-Rocket to Earth. We have sensational news: the two Thompsons are on board. They decided to spend the night in the rocket, thinking the launching was at 1.34 in the afternoon.

But this creates a grave problem! We assessed our oxygen supplies for four people; now we have six on board, not counting Snowy. Will our oxygen last out?

You hear that, you brontosaurus? All this because at your age you don't know the difference between 1.34 a.m. and 1.34 p.m.!

Anyway, I must go up and take over the controls from the automatic pilot.

Blistering barnacles! When I think that I was forbidden to smoke one single little pipe, on the pretext of saving oxygen – the very same oxygen you two come here and gulp down!... And stop snivelling like that: you're making carbon dioxide!... Thundering typhoons, goodness knows why I don't chuck you overboard, without any more ado!

I say! Come and look! Come and look!
?
!

What is it?

Here! Come and look into this strobo-scopic periscope: no human being has ever before seen this sight!

The Earth, our good old Earth, seen from over 6,000 miles!

If we have to die, it's worth it to have seen this!
Yes, I expect so... But person-ally, I'm in no hurry to die, if you don't mind!
It's a matter of opinion!.. Now I'm going to take over control of the rocket.

Moon-Rocket to Earth... This is Professor Calculus... I have taken over control... All's well on board.

Blistering barnacles, that's enough moan-ing!... Now do me a favour and take your-selves off... I have important work to do!

Go on, hop it!... Get moving!

And you'd better not come down again till I call you! ... See? ...

And that's a fact! You need to be alone to study this sort of thing.
GUIDE TO ASTRONOMY

Now, let battle commence! To work! ... To work!...

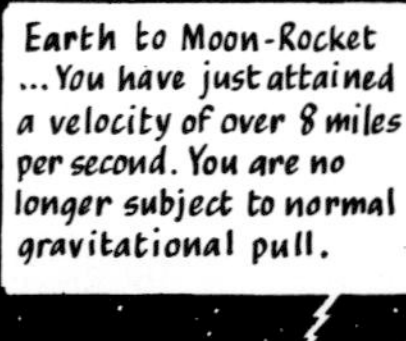
Earth to Moon-Rocket ...You have just attained a velocity of over 8 miles per second. You are no longer subject to normal gravitational pull.

Now then, here we go! We'll tackle the first chapter.

Aaaaaaaaaaah! I've learnt something al- ready!

Courage, Haddock! On to Chapter Two!

Sit down and watch. Look, there's the Moon in all her glory!

Is that really the Moon? That funny ball riddled with little holes?

It's amazing! Thompson, come and see this!

Mind out! Your stick's hooked up! For heaven's sake don't pull it!... Help!

At that moment, down below...
Here's to y-y-you, up th- th-there!

G-g-goodness g-g-gracious!... M-m-my whisky's r-r-rolled itself into a b-b-ball!... That's impossible!... Have I d-d-drunk too m-much already?

W-w-whisky, stop f-f-fooling about! Get b-b-back in my glass this m-m-minute!
?

Too m-m-much or n-n-not...a decent whisky d-d-doesn't behave l-l-like this...C-c-come here at once!

Blistering barnacles, what's the matter ?

Something's happened: Snowy doesn't usually walk upside down like that.

Look what you've done, you idiot! You've stopped the nuclear motor. The constant acceleration of our rocket created a sort of artificial gravity here inside ...

This allowed us to move about in the cabin as we do on the ground ... When the motor stops, we no longer feel the effects of gravity ... That's why we're floating like this.

Please, Professor, not a physics lecture now! ... We must start the motor again!

Wait ... I'll try to get to the controls ...

If I touch you, Snowy, you're it!

Y-y-y-you see, my dear w-w-whisky! Y-y-y-you've t-turned yourself into a b-b-ball, but I'm a p-pretty little b-b-bird! Tweet-tweet! ...
Tintin! Tintin! Where are you?

Watch out! ... I'm going to restart the nuclear motor! ... Hang on!

Carry on ... We're holding tight!

L-l-look, Snowy! ... I can even glide on my back! Th-th-this is f-fun!

Earth to Moon-Rocket ... What's going on? ... Why have you stopped the nuclear motor?

Moon-Rocket to Earth... One of the two detectives accidentally closed the motor throttle... But we've just started her up again.
It's funny, we held on very tight!
Yes, but what to?

To be on the safe side I'm issuing everyone with magnetic-soled boots...

The Professor's right. If the nuclear motor stops again for any reason, these soles will hold us down to the cabin floor. Then we shan't float about like balloons.

Unless I'm dreaming, there's Adonis!
Who's Adonis? A friend of yours living near here?

The asteroid Adonis is a dwarf planet which orbits between Mars and Jupiter. It is a rock-like mass, about a mile in diameter... Take my place and watch, while I put on my boots... but for goodness sake don't touch anything!

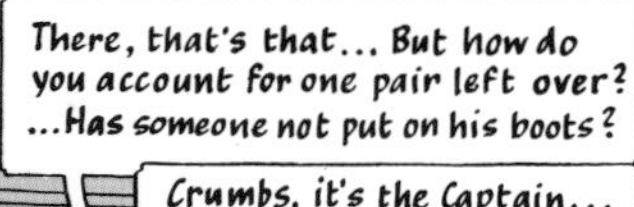
There, that's that... But how do you account for one pair left over? ...Has someone not put on his boots?

Crumbs, it's the Captain... he stayed below... I'll take them down to him.

Hello, Snowy boy. Did you get very bumped about?
So there you are Tintin!... If only you knew what happened!

And the Captain?... Where's the Captain?... I... Hello, what's that piece of paper, there on the table...?

Great snakes! It's fantastic!... He's gone out of his mind! ...Quick, the Professor must see this...

Goodness! How lucky we put these boots on. The motor's stopped again... What's the matter this time?
RRRRING RRRRING
RRRING
You see, Tintin? It's begun again!

Moon-Rocket to Earth ... For some unknown reason the outer door has just opened. The nuclear motor stopped automatically. I'm going to see why...

Here's the answer!... Read this note I just found on the table, on the deck below...
?

"I'm fed up with your rotten rocket! I'm going home to Marlinspike." Signed: Haddock. ... Goodness gracious, then it was he who... Has he gone mad?

Mad? No, I think he's just soaked himself in whisky. In any case, we must look for him. If you agree, I'll put on my space-suit and go out myself...
Of course.

A few minutes later...
Moon-Rocket to Earth... The Captain has suddenly taken it into his head to jump out of the rocket... Tintin has gone out as well, to try and help him.
Ah, there he is.

Hello Captain! Hello!... Can you hear me?
Cuckoo, it's me!

Of course I c-c-can hear you... Can you hear m-m-me?... Tweet-tweet... Tweet-tweet... You see: I've turned into a little chaffinch...

Hello, Professor... Tintin calling. I can see the Captain. He's floating about ten yards from the rocket, going at the same speed as ourselves. I'll do all I possibly can to get him back on board. ...
All right.

Me b-b-back on b-b-board your beastly flying cigar? N-n-never in my life! I'm off h-h-home to Marlinspike!
But ... Crumbs, it can't be true ...

But it is!... He's getting further away from the rocket!

Poor Captain!... Now I see: he's being pulled into orbit by Adonis!... He's lost!

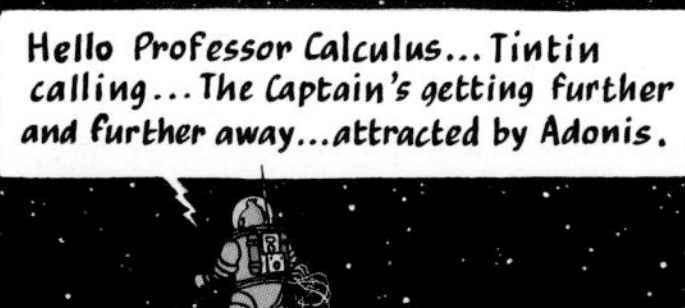
Hello Professor Calculus... Tintin calling... The Captain's getting further and further away... attracted by Adonis.

Getting further away? ... That's only to be expected... He's become a satellite of Adonis!

This is terrible!... Surely there must be something we can do?
Of course... We must inform Earth at once, and tell them Adonis has a new satellite by the name of Haddock!

Not so fast! I have a plan: you raise the retractable ladder at once, so that I can anchor myself securely. Then, start up the motor: gently at first, but getting faster and faster...
But what are you hoping to do?

To get close enough to the Captain to throw him a line, and pull him aboard.
Pull me aboard? ... Not on your life!

It's sheer madness!... But I admire you for wanting to try... I'll raise the retractable ladder as you said, and wait for your orders...

Tintin here... I'm securely anchored... You can start the motor...

All right... I ... Tintin, it's terribly risky... But, good luck, anyway! Steady now: I'm starting the motor...

?

Tintin calling... I got a terrific jolt but I managed to hold on... You are right on course...

Yes, I can see the Captain... I'll close up to him. But for goodness' sake be quick. As soon as the motor stops Adonis will start dragging us into orbit.

I'll do my best... Steady now! Stand by to cut the motor!

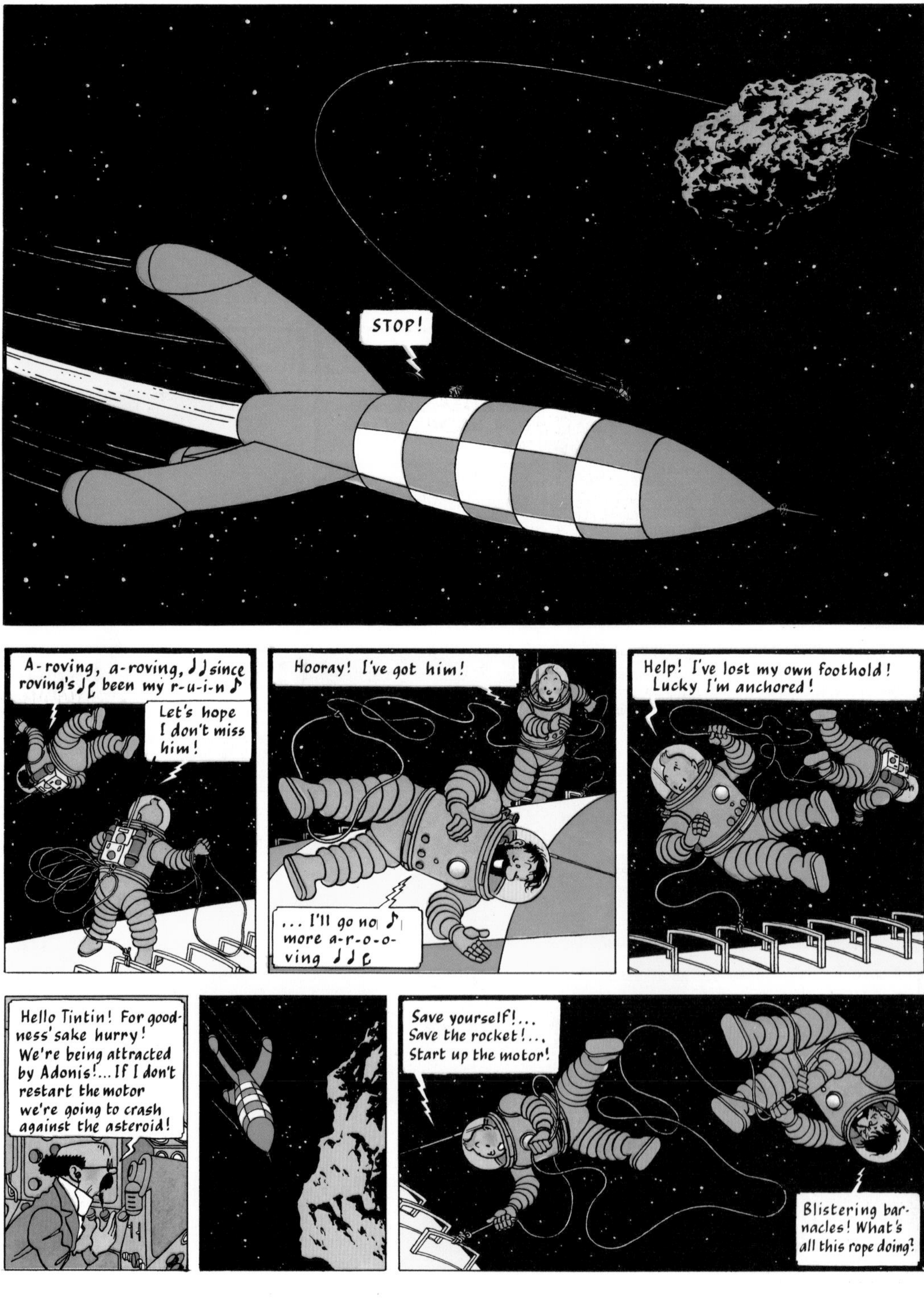

STOP!

A-roving, a-roving, ♪♪ since roving's ♪♪ been my r-u-i-n ♪
Let's hope I don't miss him!

Hooray! I've got him!
... I'll go no ♪ more a-r-o-o-ving ♪♪♪

Help! I've lost my own foothold! Lucky I'm anchored!

Hello Tintin! For goodness'sake hurry! We're being attracted by Adonis!... If I don't restart the motor we're going to crash against the asteroid!

Save yourself!... Save the rocket!... Start up the motor!
Blistering barnacles! What's all this rope doing?

?
Crumbs! What a jerk!... If only the rope doesn't break!

Hello, Tintin here... We're O.K. The rope held!

And we have put a safe distance between ourselves and Adonis! ... Now I'll stop the motor again...

Saved!... We're just floating freely once more.

Now then, don't let's waste time... Hurry up and get back on board!
Billions of blue blistering barnacles! Will you let go of me!

W-w-w-what d'you think you're doing, eh? I'm quite old enough to d-d-do as I like!... I w-want to go home, so there! ... I've had enough of this cake-walk, with whisky rolling up in a ball. We'll all end up smashed in little pieces!

Be quiet! Do you realise that all your tomfoolery has nearly cost us our lives?... Now we've had enough!... Get back inside at once! ... And try to behave yourself properly!... D'you understand?

Now, come along! And if I catch you drinking again, I'll clap you in irons for the rest of the trip!

A few minutes later...
Moon-rocket to Earth. Tintin and the Captain are safe and sound; they've just come back inside... We're re-starting the motor...

I... I'm a miserable wretch ... I had a drink... It's unpardonable... I'm terribly sorry.
That's all right... We'll forget it, but ...

OH!
Well? What is it this time?

Tintin!... Tintin!... Come quickly!... It's huge yellow caterpillars!
?

There!... There!... Look!
!
GRR

But there's no doubt about it ; this is hair!
It's hair ?
?

Yes, hair! Great snakes! The detectives!
The detectives? What do you mean?

Oh dear, it's what I feared : another attack!

Yes, another attack... the trouble they developed after eating those strange pills in the Arabian desert.[1] ... They've taken some medicine; we must wait till it works...
They always have to make themselves conspicuous, the jelly-fishes!

You poor fellows!... Are you in much pain?
Fortunately not: none at all.

OW!... YOW!...YEOW!
YOW!... OW!...

?
Oh, it's Snowy!

Snowy, let go!... No?... Then just you wait!

What are you going to do?
Fetch a pair of scissors!

There!

For the time being, until your medicine takes effect, I'll cut this shock of hair for you. But first let's go below; it will be easier down there...

Here, give me the scissors. I'll shear these merino lambs myself!
Oh?... As you please...

Earth to Moon-Rocket... Attention! ..Attention! ...

Earth to Moon-Rocket... Stand by... The turning operation will have to be made in twenty minutes' time.

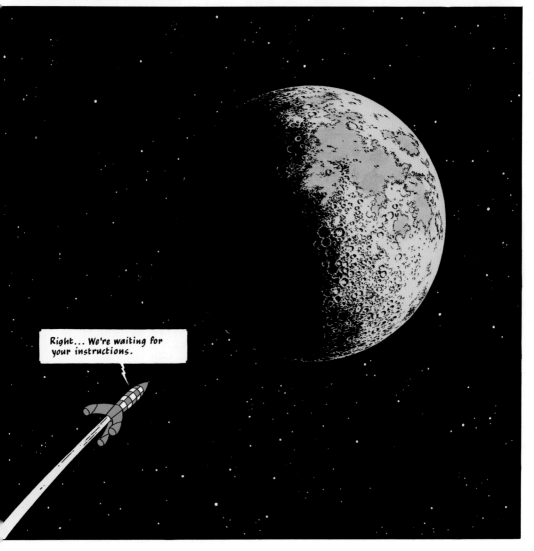

Right... We're waiting for your instructions.

So now we're going to turn round... What's this latest acrobatic? Why not loop-the-loop, or do a roll, or go into a spin, thundering typhoons?!...
Wait, I'll explain to you...

BEEP...BEEP...

BEEP...BEEP...BEEP...
What in the world's that?
That?... It's a radar signal - a warning that a large meteorite is heading towards us.

BEEP...BEEP...BEEP...
Now we shall see whether or not the automatic system I installed works properly.
And how will you know if it works?

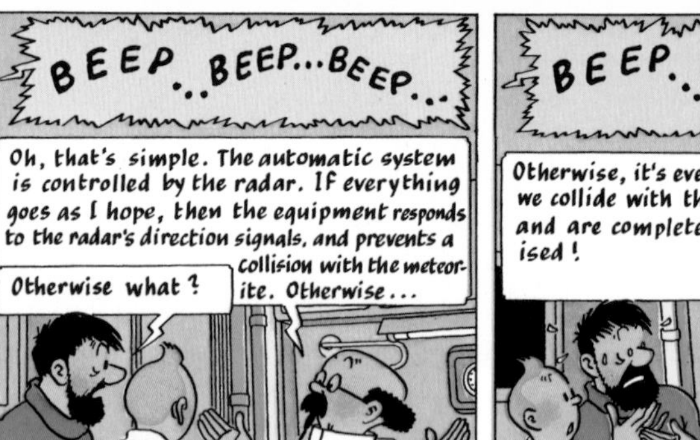
BEEP...BEEP...BEEP...
Oh, that's simple. The automatic system is controlled by the radar. If everything goes as I hope, then the equipment responds to the radar's direction signals, and prevents a collision with the meteorite. Otherwise...
Otherwise what?
BEEP...BEEP...
Otherwise, it's even simpler: we collide with the meteorite, and are completely pulverised!

BEEP...BEEP...BEEP...
But don't worry! We'll soon know!

Whew!... The danger's passed!... I can breathe again. I don't mind telling you, I was very frightened.
Would we really have been smashed to smithereens?

Not only that! Far more serious!... I can tell you now: if my theories hadn't worked out, I'd have had to begin all my calculations over again.

A few minutes later...
And when anyone asks me later on: "What was your job in the rocket?" I'll say, "Me? I was the hairdresser!"

A mop like this doesn't need a pair of scissors to cut it...

...it needs pruning-shears, ten thousand thundering typhoons, or a lawn-mower!

Whew! There's one cropped! Next gentleman, please!... What?... Is His Highness not satisfied?
Ha! ha! ha! ha!... My poor fellow! If you could see yourself!
?

Go on, laugh! Laugh!... If you imagine you look more dignified than your esteemed friend, you've got another think coming!

And none of this would have happened, thundering typhoons, if you'd been able to tell the blistering difference between 1 p.m. and 1 a.m.!

There, that's finished!... Look at my hands now!... All covered in blisters!
?

Well, what is it? His lordship isn't pleased?... What more do you want?... A shampoo and set?... Or would you rather I put it in curlers?
OH!

Look!... There!...
?!
Ha! ha! ha! My poor fellow! If you could see yourself!

Professor!...
Professor!

Professor, we simply must do something for the Thompsons ... Their hair grows as fast as I can cut it, and ...
Ssh!... Earth's calling us.

Earth to Moon-Rocket... You have three minutes to go before the turning operation.
Right.

I didn't get a chance to tell you about this manoeuvre... What do you think will happen if we go on heading for the Moon, with our rocket pointing directly at it?
We shall end up by arriving, I suppose.

Of course, but like a missile. Travelling as we are, at such a terrific speed, we would crash on the Moon, and that would be the end of us all... Is that really what you want?
Me?...

Listen!... There's only one thing I want, blistering barnacles! To be able to breathe God's good air, instead of air out of a tin!... And to smoke my pipe!... That's all I want!

Good! Now, what do we do to prevent ourselves crashing on the Moon?... Quite simply, we turn our rocket completely round, nose to tail. To do this, first we cut out the main motor, and start up an engine giving directional thrust... Once the rocket has turned round, the exhaust from our nuclear motor will brake our descent. If all goes well, this will allow us to land quite gently on the Moon... You follow me?...
In fact, if I understand you correctly, it's the same procedure as for launching, but exactly the other way round.

Earth to Moon-Rocket... Stand by... Two minutes to go before stopping the main motor...

Get ready, everybody... And Captain, unless you want to start flapping about like a butterfly when the motor stops, hurry and put on your magnetic boots.

Oh Columbus! And my boots are down below!... Quick, I'll put them on...

One minute to go...

Thirty seconds to go...

Twenty seconds to go...

Ten seconds to go... Nine ... eight... seven... six... five... four... three... two... one... ZERO

I say, Captain!... Did you have time to get your boots on?

Just... I've only got to do them up...
?

?
!

Earth to Moon-Rocket... Stand by to start up the directional thrust... Ten seconds to go... nine... eight... seven... six... five ... four... three... two... one... ZERO.

Stand by to cut the directional thrust... Ten seconds to go... nine... eight... seven... six... five... four... three... two... one... ZERO.

Stand by to start up the main motor ... Ten seconds to go ... nine... eight... seven... six... five ... four... three... two... one... ZERO.

Moon-Rocket to Earth... The turning operation...

... was entirely successful!

... We are now in a position to reduce our speed gradually, and to land safely on the Moon...
Well, carry on, my friends! Happy Moon-landing! Ha! ha! ha!

I say, boss, do you really think they'll land on the Moon?
Ha! ha! I'm hoping so!... But whether they'll ever come back, that's another story!

I... er... don't understand... Why?... Is it....?
Sh! Top secret!... You'll see later... Ah, there's their radio coming in again...
Earth calling..

Earth to Moon-Rocket... This is your present situation... You have another 88,000 miles to go... You are on the estimated course. You are gradually slowing down.

A little later...
Earth to Moon-Rocket... You have only 31,000 miles to go... In 40 minutes' time you should set the automatic pilot to land on the Moon at the selected place...

Moon-Rocket to Earth... Right! We're just going to have a meal now. Then we'll prepare for the Moon-landing.

Yes, my friends. If all goes well, in half an hour's time our rocket will come to rest on the Moon, on the spot I have chosen - almost beside the Sea of Nectar... Thank you, Tintin.

The seaside?... Why, that's wonderful. ... It's ages since we went to the seaside, isn't it, Thompson?
It jolly well is!... But I didn't know there was a seaside resort on the Moon... Did you know that, Captain?

Of course!... Everybody knows! ...I even heard that they need two Punch-and-Judy men on the pier. You'd fit the job perfectly.

"Lunar seas" was the ancient name for the dark patches astronomers saw on the Moon. We still use the names, like the Sea of Nectar and the Ocean of Storms. But you won't find a drop of water anywhere there.

The Moon is covered with high-walled depressions called craters. About 90,000 have been counted. Some are only a few hundred yards across. Others, like Bailly, measure 150 miles...
Gracious! Craters are hot places inside volcanoes. We'll have to take care that the rocket doesn't fall into one!

Don't worry; most lunar craters aren't live volcanoes. It's just the name given to them. As a matter of fact, we are going to land inside the crater Hipparchus, which is about 90 miles across...

No! no! a thousand times no!... I'm not letting that pass!
?

What on earth's the matter ?
This... this man has insulted us, and we demand an apology !
Me ?... I insulted you? ... Me ?

Yes, you sir!... Did you or did you not say that they need two Punch-and-Judy men on the pier, and we'd do perfectly for the job? ... Isn't that insulting us ?
Quite right!... This man has apologised to us, and we demand an insult!

No! you great oaf! You're back to front!
Oh?... You mean... we've insulted this man and we owe him an apology? ...

All right: I take back what I said. They don't need two Punch-and-Judy men on the pier: so you can't have the job... Does that satisfy you?
Yes, we're satisfied.
To be precise: we certainly are!

Yes, that's all right ...quite all right. They don't need two Punch-and-Judy men, so...
So we can't have the job... It's simple, isn't it?

My friends! Calm down, please! Are the first men to land on the Moon going to begin by quarrelling ?

Let us not forget that we are in mortal peril! We must keep our heads... Let us be friends... and restrain our tempers... Come gentlemen, make it up now... Then everyone must go to his bunk.

Everyone to his bunk?... But Professor, there are six of us, and only four bunks... Naturally I can give up mine to one of our friends here, but...
Certainly not!

Your place is at the radio: you must keep in touch with the Earth for as long as possible. I'll look after these two.

There are two spare mattresses: spread them out on the floor and lie down.
It's kind of you, but we aren't sleepy.

Sleepy or not, I say you're to lie down! That's an order, d'you hear?... An order!

It's time I went to help Wolff make final preparations for the Moon-landing.

Earth to Moon-Rocket,... Stand by... Stand by... You are only 3,750 miles from the Moon...

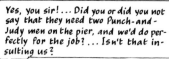

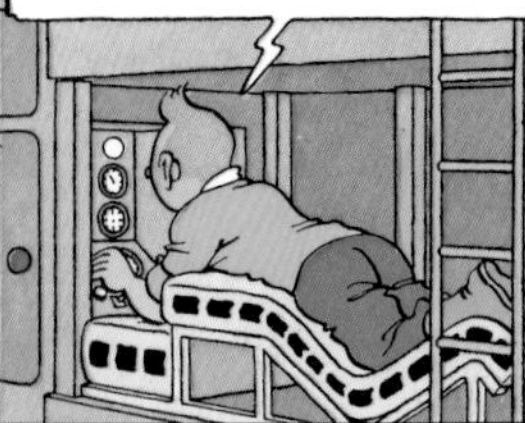
Moon-Rocket to Earth... Right ... We are making final preparations... The Professor is now setting the automatic pilot ...

Another seven points East... No, that's too much... One point West, Wolff... There, that's it! The rocket is now heading right for the centre of the crater Hipparchus.

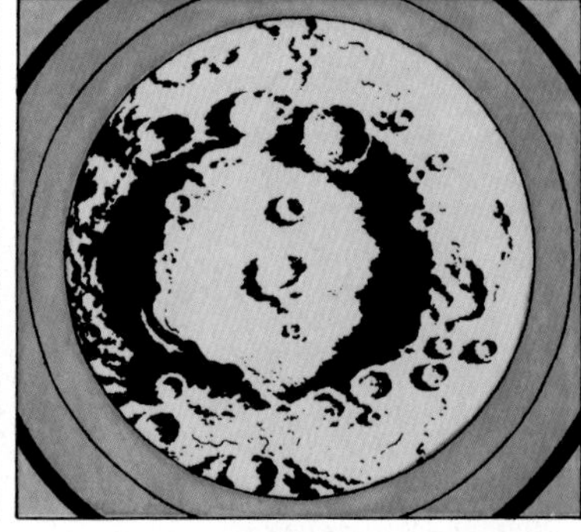

Here, Snowy!

You see, you'll feel much...

...better here while the rocket... I say! What do you think you're doing?

Us?... We're going to lie down like we've been told to! ... But my colleague and I don't sleep in our clothes.

Blistering barnacles! You don't have to sleep, you prize purple jelly-fishes! You were told to lie down. That's all! So jump to it!

And get a move on, you dunder-headed Ethelreds! ... If the Professor catches you still around, he'll probably maroon you on an empty planet ... Look, here he comes now.

Ah, everybody lying down? That's good. You must come now, Wolff.

Moon-Rocket to Earth... All's well. We are ready. The automatic pilot is set towards the middle of the crater Hipparchus. We're all lying on our bunks, waiting.

Moon-Rocket to Earth ...The nuclear motor has just stopped, and the auxiliary engine has taken over.

It's amazing!... It's tremendous!... It's incredible! Just think: in a few minutes' time, either we'll be walking on the Moon, or we'll all be dead. It's marvellous!

Moon-Rocket to Earth... Tintin calling... We are beginning to feel the effects of slackening speed...

The rocket is being shaken by slight vibrations... We are lying flat on our bunks... It's an effort to make the least movement...

Our ears are ringing... The vibrations are getting stronger and stronger... The crushing sensation is worse... It's getting difficult to breathe...

We're being crushed into our bunks... by an intolerable... weight ... can't move now... The Professor... blacked out ... I ... think... ... I think...

... my head... will... burst! ... My eyes... I... I'm sure ... they'll pop... out of their ...sockets... I ... My heart ... Oh, my heart...

Hello... The Cap... the Captain... blacked out too... Ooh, this is agony... The... the rocket... shaking ... in every rivet... Let's hope... Let's hope... it won't... Oooh!

.......crrr.... ...fttt.... ....crrr.....

That's all... Nothing more!... Poor Tintin must have blacked out as well ...Oh, this silence is unbearable!

WOOW OW OW OW!!

WOO WO WOWOW!!!

That was the dog howling for the dead!... Then he must have passed out too.

Earth to Moon-Rocket... ...Are you receiving me? ...Earth to Moon-Rocket...

Crrr... crrr... crrr...
Earth to Moon-Rocket... Are you receiving me?..

Earth to Moon-Rocket... Are you receiving me?...

Earth to Moon-Rocket ... Are you receiving me?...
By Lucifer! Let's hope nothing has happened to them!

Earth to Moon-Rocket...
Earth to Moon-Rocket...
Are you receiving me?...

Something must be wrong... We've been calling them for more than half an hour, and still no answer ... Try again...
Earth to Moon-Rocket... Are you receiving me?...

Moon-Rocket to Earth... Moon-Rocket to Earth... Receiving you loud and clear...
They're alive!... They're alive!...
Hooray!

This is Cuthbert Calculus speaking to you from the Moon!!... Success!... Success!!... We're all safe and sound... We couldn't get through to you before; the radio was damaged. It must have been the vibrations that shook the rocket... Hello Earth... Did you get that?

Message received ... But it sounds as if the vibrations haven't stopped yet: we can hear strange rumbling noises...

I... er... It's nothing: don't worry... You can hear...er ... the two detectives snoring! ...They haven't woken up yet.
ZZZZ...
ZZZZ...

Now we are going to disembark from the rocket... The honour has fallen to the youngest among us: we have chosen Tintin to be the first human being to set foot on the Moon... He's just gone down to put on his equipment. He'll give you a direct account of his first impressions, so I'll hand you over to him... That's all for now...

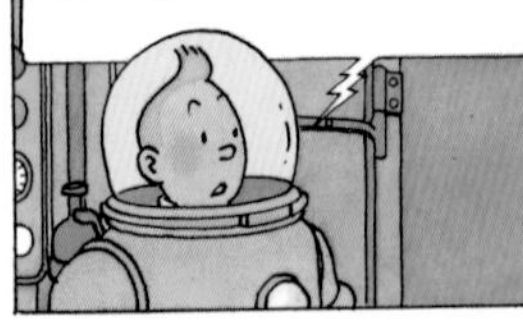
This is Tintin speaking. I've just put on my space-suit and am now standing in the air-lock. They're just going to reduce the pressure to a vacuum inside here. Captain Haddock is in charge. I'm waiting for his final instructions.

Captain Haddock speaking... Pressure zero.. Retractable ladder in position... Are you ready? Stand by!...I'm opening the door!

It's a solemn moment...The outside door is swinging slowly on its hinges and...

OOOOOOH!...
?
?

Oooh! What a fantastic sight!

It's... How can I describe it?... It's a nightmare land, a place of death, horrifying in its desolation ...Not a tree, not a flower, not a blade of grass. ... Not a bird, not a sound, not a cloud. In the inky black sky there are thousands of stars...

... but they are motionless, frozen; they don't twinkle in the way that makes them look so alive to us on Earth.

Now I'm descending the ladder which runs down the side of the rocket.

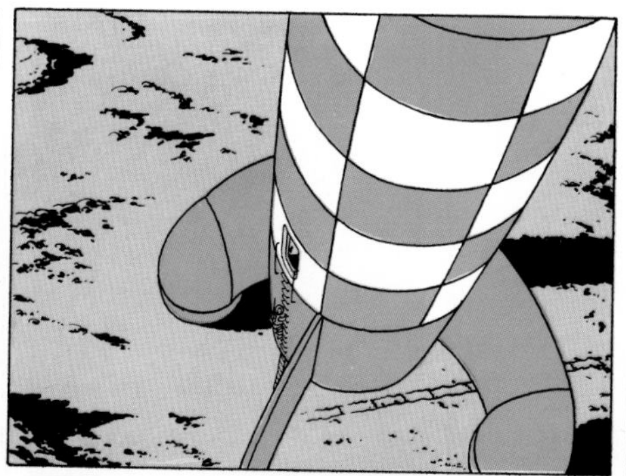

Only a few more rungs. ... Now three... Now two... Now only one... This is it!

This is it!... I've walked a few steps!... For the first time in the history of mankind there is an EXPLORER ON THE MOON!

But already I'm not alone...There's the Captain coming to join me.

On the Moon!...It's terrific!...I'm walking on the Moon!...I'm walking...running... jumping!

?
?

Good heavens, what a leap!

Ha! ha! ha! You see, Captain! On the Moon, gravity is actually six times less than on the Earth.
And I knew that all the time, thundering typhoons!...But I'd completely forgotten.

There! Look at the Earth!... Our good old Earth. It looks four times bigger than the Moon does, when we see it at home.
Let's hope we'll be able to get back there one day!

Hello Tintin...Here's Snowy coming to join you. I'll follow him down.
WOOAAAH!...

You see. There was no need to get so excited.
That's what you think!

Anyway, I'm not sorry to have a chance to stretch my legs!

Golly! now I've taken off like a dragon-fly!

The Moon!...Just imagine, walking calmly along on the Moon!... Old Calculus is an incredible fellow!

?
?

What happened?... Was that an earthquake?
A Moon-quake, more likely, but...

Great snakes!... Look there!
Thundering typhoons! What in the world's that?...

A meteorite! Look, a meteorite! It's just fallen on the exact spot where we were a moment ago... and exploded!
Exploded? But I didn't hear a sound!

Naturally not. There's no air on the Moon, so there's no noise... And that's why the meteorite came down intact, too. Back at home, on the Earth, the friction of the atmosphere would have made it white hot. So it would have disintegrated before reaching the ground, making what we generally call a "shooting star".

Anyway, if those tycoons on the lunar development corporation imagine that this sort of welcome will attract tourists to the Moon, they'll have to think again.

Ah, hello my friends!... This is incredible!... It's fantastic!... We're on the Moon! D'you realise that?
Oh, so there you are!

Just take a look there!... A little bit closer, and you'd have been able to throw away our return tickets!
A meteorite! How marvellous!

Oh, so you think that's marvellous, do you? When we'd have been as flat as pancakes!
What do you expect? It's an occupational hazard!

Exactly, blistering barnacles! But this isn't my occupation! Thundering typhoons, I'm a sailor!... And on board ship, at least you don't run the risk of bits of sky falling down all over the place, every time you bat an eyelid!
Maybe!... But just try coming to the Moon by boat!

Still, that's not the point. We must set to work. Come along and unload the cargo. We must start at once. Wolff has already got everything prepared.

But I wonder what he's waiting for. ... Hello, Wolff... This is Calculus calling. Can you hear me, Wolff?... Hello?

Good heavens, what's happening?... The ladder... The door... Captain, look!

The ladder's retracted!...The door is shut!... What in the world does this mean?
Hello, Wolff?

Hello, Wolff, hello? Blistering barnacles, what are you playing at up there? Hello, hello! ... Hello Wolff? Thundering typhoons, are you going to answer me?

Hello? Hello?...Ah, there's the ladder again. And the door has been reopened.

You certainly gave us a fright, Wolff! ... We thought for a moment that the rocket was suddenly going to take off and return to Earth, leaving us stuck here in this delightful place!

I'm terribly sorry... I ... Just a mistake... So stupid... I wasn't thinking ...

Never mind, forget about it!... Now Wolff, we're going to discharge the cargo. The Captain's coming up to help you get the crates out of the holds. Tintin and I will stay down here.

It's quite a simple job. Each crate is bound with steel wires connected to a central ring. You only have to slip the ring over the hook on the pulley-block.
Right!... I'll go up and join Wolff.

Moon-Rocket to Earth... Calculus calling... We've just been discharging the cargo. Everything is going very smoothly.

The hours go by...

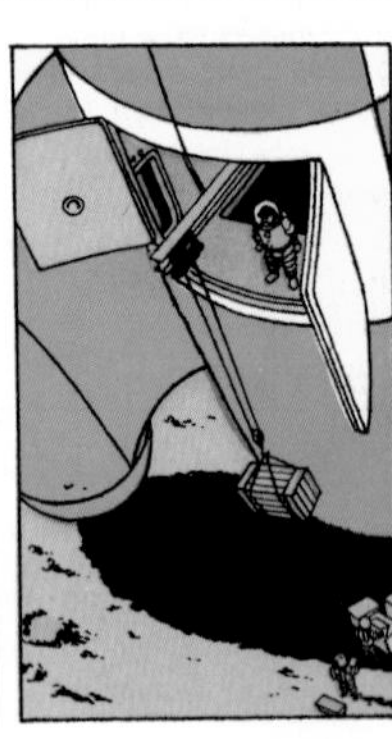

There... As far as the cargo's concerned, we'll soon have finished. But we've still got to unload the reconnaissance tank.

Hello, Captain? Next one please.

?
... heavens! Mind out!

Young man, would you be kind enough to explain the meaning of this ridiculous prank?

Billions of blue blistering barnacles! I'd thank Tintin if I were you. Without him you'd have been smashed to pulp!

Look, Professor. Was I wrong to push you over?

The wires have parted. Just look there; they've been worn through by friction. It must have been caused by the vibrations to the rocket towards the end of the journey.

We certainly had a bit of luck! Shall we carry on, Captain? But this time be sure to check the wires.

And how! I'll make doubly sure!

I say, Wolff, we're going to carry on... By Christopher, Wolff, what's the matter?

I... I don't know... I felt dizzy... suddenly... I thought I was going to faint. Perhaps it's my heart... I ... It'll go: I feel better already.

Don't worry, Wolff; probably it's only fatigue. And perhaps your oxygen supply is badly adjusted. Go and lie down. In fact, we'll all follow suit.

A few minutes later...

Moon-Rocket to Earth. We've just come back on board for a bit of a rest. Meanwhile the two detectives have gone out to have a turn at exploring.

Imagine! Here we are, strolling on the surface of the Moon, where the hand of man has never set foot!
Hm!... Really never?

Stop, my dear fellow! Stop!

A crevasse! By jove, we must watch our step!

For goodness' sake be careful!

!
?
Did you see that? It's amazing! A standing jump, too!

It's your turn now. Come on, don't be scared!

What d'you think of that, eh? Even further than you, old man!

I've had an idea. Hold my hand. We're going to dance a little ballet!
A ballet?... All right, if you want to..

Ha! ha! ha!
Ha! ha! ha!
Ha ha ha! ha ha ha!
Come on, be serious! Supposing people saw us!

People!...Ha! ha! ... PEOPLE!
Well why not?

You talk as if we were in a busy street... But there aren't any people on the Moon, my poor friend!
And how do they know there's no one here if no one's ever been?

?
Besides, look there!

Well?... You see? ... What did I tell you?
Footsteps!... There's someone else besides us on the Moon!

Hello, this is Thompson... with a 'p' as in Percival... Calling Moon-Rocket...
Moon-Rocket here ...Calculus speaking. We are receiving you.

Thompson calling...We've made a sensational discovery...Sen-sa-tion-al, d'you hear? Listen to this: there are people on the Moon!
What sort of fairy-tale is that? People? Other people?... Nonsense!

But there are! We've discovered footsteps!
Footsteps? But great sunspots, they're obviously footsteps made by one of us.

They can't be made by ONE of us: there are TWO sets of footsteps!
Quite right!

Then they're footsteps made by two of us, nitwit!... I expect you've gone back on your tracks, and those are your own footmarks!

Great Scotland Yard! Have we been going round in circles, following our own tracks - as in the desert?
Definitely not! Because there are two sets of tracks, and we're alone!

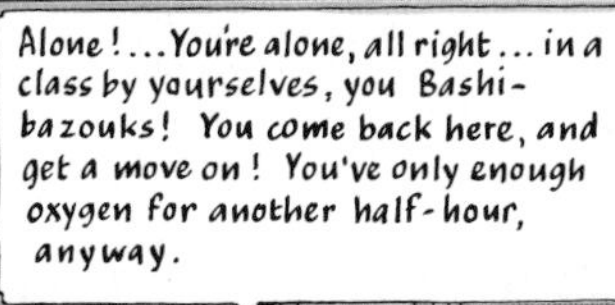
Alone!...You're alone, all right... in a class by yourselves, you Bashi-bazouks! You come back here, and get a move on! You've only enough oxygen for another half-hour, anyway.

All right, all right, we're coming... Since you despise our scientific contributions...

Perhaps it's silly, but I wonder... Those footsteps they saw... What if there are other men on the Moon? D'you think that's absolutely impossible?

Impossible?...Theoretically, no. If we were able to get here, then others could too. But as far as I'm concerned, I'm certain we are the first - and the only people - to land on the Moon.
Oh, good.

They can say what they like in there... We'll see who's right in the end.
Yes, yes... Patience!

A few minutes later . . .

Gentlemen, our plan was to stay on the Moon for a whole lunar day - that's equivalent to fourteen terrestrial days. But our oxygen supplies were intended for four people and one dog, and not for six people, which is our present number. So we shall have to restrict our stay to six days.

We must therefore hasten our work. While Wolff and I set up our observational instruments, Tintin and the Captain will unload the components of our reconnaissance tank and assemble it. Is that agreed? Right then, gentlemen, let's get to work!

EXTRACT FROM THE LOG BOOK BY PROFESSOR CALCULUS

3rd June - 2345 hrs. (G.M.T.). Unloading of cargo completed. Wolff and I have started to install the observatory. Ceased work at 2200 hrs. Captain Haddock and Tintin have begun assembling the tank.
4th June - 0830 hrs. Operations commenced at 0400 hrs (G.M.T.). Telescope mounted. Cameras in position. Theodolite in workin order.

Moon to Earth... Calculus calling... The optical instruments and cameras are ready for use. We are beginning our observational work.

Observe away, my friends. You do that! Your discoveries will be vastly interesting ... TO US! Ha! ha! ha! ha!

EXTRACT FROM THE LOG BOOK BY PROFESSOR CALCULUS

4th June - 2150 hrs. (G.M.T.). Wolff and I spent the day studying cosmic rays, and making astronomical observations. Our findings have been entered progressively in Special Record Books Nos. I and II. The Captain and Tintin have nearly finished assembling the tank.
5th June - 1920 hrs. (G.M.T.). Half an hour ago the Captain and Tintin pronounced the tank ready for use.

Moon to Earth... Calculus calling... The tank is ready. We're going to make the first trials. Tintin will be in charge. He's just entering the turret.

He has just secured the hatch. Now they are filling the insulated cabin with air. When this is done they can remove their space-suits; then Tintin will take the controls and the Captain will act as look-out.

Ah, there's Tintin's head showing throug the multiplex cockpit cover. He's smiling at me and signalling that everything's in order.

And there's the Captain. Like Tintin, he's signalling to us that all's well. He's wearing his head-phones and ...

Hello, Haddock calling... Ready for departure ... Hello there, Tintin, weigh the anchor!

Good luck!

O.K... Off we go!

!

Billions of blue blistering barnacles, Tintin! Couldn't you cast off more smoothly?

I'm sorry. It's the first time I've driven this sort of machine...

... but don't you think I've learnt a lot already?

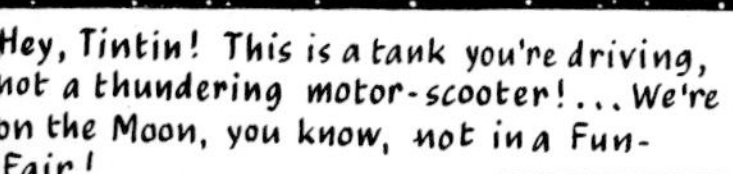
Hey, Tintin! This is a tank you're driving, not a thundering motor-scooter! ... We're on the Moon, you know, not in a Fun-Fair!

I'm doing my best, but...

Steady! Hang on tight!

Tintin calling... Apart from the bumps, everything's fine.

u won't catch me being a regular pas-
nger in your blistering taxi!

HELP!

Stop, Tintin, for heaven's sake! Stop!... This is ghastly! My microphone's bust... Tintin can't hear me!

Great snakes! A crevasse!... Stop!

Crumbs! That was a near thing! A few more inches and we'd have plunged into that chasm!

Blistering barnacles, it's a mere detail that I cracked my head against that cover again!... But we've had enough! We're going home! We know now that the tank goes well... and that crash helmets are indispensable!
I agree. I'll reverse, and we'll go back to Base.

EXTRACT FROM THE LOG BOOK BY PROFESSOR CALCULUS

*6th June - 1340 hrs. (G.M.T.)
This is a day that will go down in the annals of Science. We have succeeded in making direct measurement of the constant of solar radiation, and fixing exactly the limits of the solar spectrum in the ultraviolet. An hour ago, at 1235 precisely, Wolff, the Captain, Tintin and Snowy set off on a reconnaissance trip in the tank, towards the crater Ptolemaeus.*

Tank calling Base. All's going well on board.

Whew! It's hot under this flowerpot! I'm positively melting!

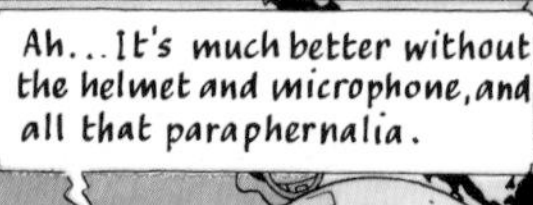
Ah... It's much better without the helmet and microphone, and all that paraphernalia.

I say!... What's that I can see over there?

STOP!

Right, I'm drawing up.

Look there, over on your left: at the foot of the cliff!
?
?

See down there, behind that finger of rock...
It looks like the entrance to a cave.

That's just what I thought. We'd better have a closer look at it.
Right. I'll go across. Are you coming too, Captain?
O.K., I'm with you.

Hello, Wolff... You're quite right. It's definitely the entrance to a cave.

It remains to be seen where it leads to. Come on. I'll switch on my lamp.

Blistering barnacles! I've done a good many things in my time...but never lunar spelaeology!

We're in a proper cathedral!

Stalagmites and stalactites... This proves that at some period there was water on the Moon.

Snowy, Snowy, don't go far ahead. Be careful, and stay close to us.
He doesn't seem to realise that I'm grown up! Honestly! What does he take me for? Granny's little lap-dog?

WOOOAH!
!

Great snakes! A crevasse! He must have fallen in!

Quick, Captain. Hold tight! I'll try and shine a light down.

The crevasse bends sharply. I can't see far. Snowy! Snowy!

Quickly, Captain! Undo your rope and secure it to a rock.
But you aren't really going to...

Yes, yes. We must do all we can to try and save poor Snowy. Hurry! Tie me an absolutely firm knot.
There... But it's sheer madness...

All right?
All right?

For heaven's sake, Tintin, be careful! You know what it'll mean if you smash your oxygen pipe.
Yes, I know.

Ah! I'm standing on a sort of ledge... Snowy! Snowy!

Tintin, be sensible: come back! It's quite useless. You don't really imagine he could have survived a fall like that?... You must come back!
No, I'm going on. Perhaps he's only hurt.

The crevasse is widening. I'm still going down.

Oh! The rope is too short. I've come to the end. I can't go down any further.

You see, you donkey! Blistering barnacles, come on up!

You're right. I'll come up... Snowy!... Snowy!

Captain... Captain... I think I saw something move. I'm letting go of the rope. It can't be far to the bottom.

You're crazy! Tintin, don't do that!

Into the hands of Fate!

Great snakes!... Ice!

Snowy!... You're there! Nothing broken? But what's the matter? You aren't answering... Oh, now I see: your radio isn't working.

Hello, Captain... I've found Snowy! He's safe and sound. But his radio's smashed. I'll climb back up to the rope.
My dear Tintin, you don't imagine you can stand up on this skating-rink, do you?

You see? What did I tell you?

Crumbs! How can I climb this icy slope?... There's only one way to do it: by cutting steps with a chunk of rock. Oh well, to work!

Hello, Captain... Untie the rope and let it down as far as possible... When I manage to reach it I'll tie Snowy on, and you can pull him up. ... Then I'll follow.
O.K.

Here we are at last!

Hello, Captain. Let out more rope: it isn't down far enough for me to tie it round Snowy.
Right.

That's done it.

A few minutes later...

Hello Tintin... That's it... Snowy is safe now.
?

Hello Tintin... I've secured a heavy stone to the end of the rope. I'm letting it down ...

All right, Captain. But hurry: it's beginning to get difficult to breathe.

I'm almost at the end. Can you see the rope?

No, I can't see it. Do please hurry!

Blistering barnacles, what's up? The rope's somehow got shorter than it was just now.

Oh!... I can't feel the weight of the stone any longer... It must have come off, or else it's wedged somewhere. Quick, start again...

Meanwhile...
Hello, Wolff... Well, what news?

Wolff here... Still no sign. It's more than half an hour since they went into the cave. I'm beginning to wonder if... Ah, there they are!

Heavens! Tintin's staggering—he looks pretty groggy. The Captain's almost carrying him. Hello, Captain, is he hurt?

No. But he's just about reached the end of his tether, poor lad.

Saved! My friends, they're saved!

Tank calling Base. The Captain and Tintin are back on board. The Captain's taken over command as Tintin is completely exhausted. We're returning post-haste!

Some hours later...
Moon-Rocket to Earth... Calculus calling. The tank is back, but is going off at once. This time the Captain, Thomson and Thompson, and myself will be on board. Our trip will last about forty-eight hours. Our aim is to do a more careful survey of the caves discovered by Tintin; they may contain rich deposits of uranium, or radium.

Aha! I have a feeling that Operation Ulysses is entering a decisive phase. We're going to have some fun!

A few minutes later...
Tank calling Base. We're leaving now. Goodbye!

Moon-Rocket calling... Tintin here. Good luck and good hunting!... And don't leave us alone for too long!

Calculus here... Don't worry, Tintin. We'll be back in forty-eight hours.

I don't know why, by thunder, but something tells me it would be wiser to turn back!

Goodbye... See you soon. I'm going to start mending the radios on our space-suits. Goodbye!

Goodbye, Tintin!... Goodbye, Wolff!

It's time for a meal. I... er... I'll go down to the stores to find something for lunch...
A good idea, too. I'm dog tired of waiting.

Would you like me to go?
No, no... er... don't you bother. I'll go myself.

It's strange how Wolff has altered. At first, in the Centre at Sprodj, he was smiling and happy... He's not the same man at all now. What can have changed him so?
I never cared for him much. And I've got a good nose!

A few minutes later...
There... I've found all we need.
If only it were a tin of bones!

Oh, bother!
Why, what's the matter?
?

Er... nothing much. I forgot to bring any tinned milk... I'll have to go down to the stores again.

Certainly not. This time it's my turn to go.
Oh, all right. Thank you. It's very kind of you.

You'll see the box right in front of you as you go in.
Good.

He's going down! It's too late to do anything!... Now he's at the bottom... He's going into the hold...

24

Aha, my young friend. You never expected that one day Colonel Jorgen would come as far as the Moon for his revenge, did you?[1]

Wolff! Hi, Wolff! I've done it. You can come...

I... I'm coming.

Good heavens... you... you haven't... after all... too hard?

No, no, don't worry. I've just... put him to sleep! And now, Wolff, back we go to Earth.
What?... What do you mean? Without waiting for the others?

Without waiting for the others – of course! Tell me: how soon can the rocket be ready for take-off?
No, we can't do that!... Marooning them on the Moon will condemn them to a hideous death. It would be an atrocious crime!

Tut-tut! Cut out the fine words, my dear Wolff! And cut out the noble sentiments, too! We're leaving, and that's that!
No! I refuse to do it! I won't be a party to such a monstrous deed!

My dear Wolff, listen to me! Supposing we wait for the others to come back, and overpower them one by one as they leave the air-lock. Right... Then, we set off for the Earth with our prisoners... But the oxygen ... what about the oxygen, eh Wolff?

Supplies were provided for four people: we are seven. So? It's too easy: we'll all be dead before the end of the journey. Is that what you want?... Well? Answer me!... Good... Now you're seeing sense!... Come with me. We'll go up and prepare for departure.

Ah, here's Tintin coming up again.

!
?

Wooah!... Wooah!... Grrr... Bang!... Thump!

Hello, Tintin... Tank calling... What's all that hullabaloo?

Hello, Wolff here... I ...er... It's nothing. ...Tintin went below ...and Snowy, you see ...Snowy wanted to follow him. But it's all over now...

How right you are! It's over for good!

Why... What are you doing? How can that poor animal do you any harm?

You never can tell, Wolff! This wretched mongrel could make trouble for us later on.

So that's that! And now, my friend, you're going to cook me a nice hot meal. For eight days I've been living on dry sandwiches, and I've had enough of them! So get moving!... And don't waste any time!

Then we set off for the Earth. Ha! ha! ha! I'd like to see their faces when they find the rocket's gone!... Killing!

Is that food coming, Wolff? I'm as hungry as a lion!

In a minute... I... Not long now...
Hello! Tank calling Base!
?

We've had a breakdown. The motor batteries are flat. A short-circuit, I expect. The Captain is just connecting the small emergency batteries, so that we can get back to Base.

By Lucifer! They're coming back! We must take off immediately! Leave your pots and pans, Wolff... We're on our way, at once!

At once? It's impossible. The motor has to be prepared for at least half an hour.
Fool! Couldn't you have remembered that sooner? Well, hurry! What are you waiting for?

Meanwhile...

Crumbs, what am I doing here?... And... Oooh my head!... But what... I'm tied up!! ... What's happened to me?
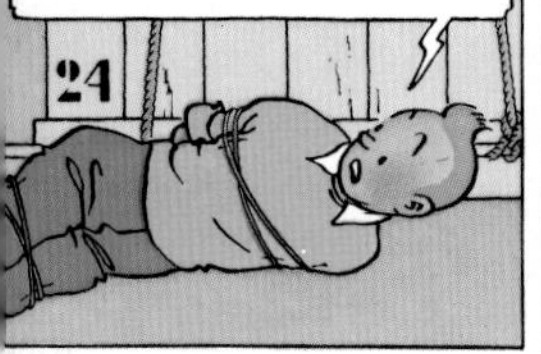
I don't understand at all. I... Why, what's that humming noise? Good heavens! It's the motor... But then... then... the rocket's going to take off...
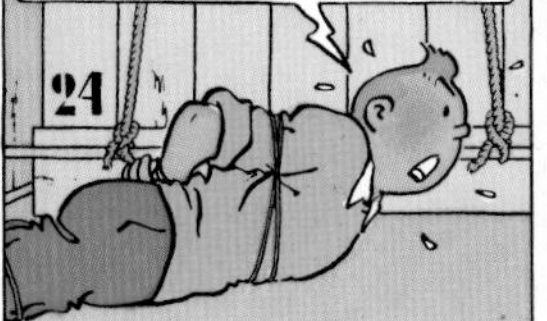
But where are the others? Prisoners like myself? But come to think of it... Poor devils! They went off in the tank... Are they going to be left on the Moon? Wolff! Wolff! HELP!

Tank calling Base... We're returning at reduced speed. We can see the rocket... Can you hear me?...

Ready yet?
Another quarter of an hour.

This is Tank calling Moon-Rocket... Are you receiving me? Answer please.
How odd. The ladder has retracted. And the door is closed. What can be the meaning of that?

Well Wolff? Can we go?
No, not yet.

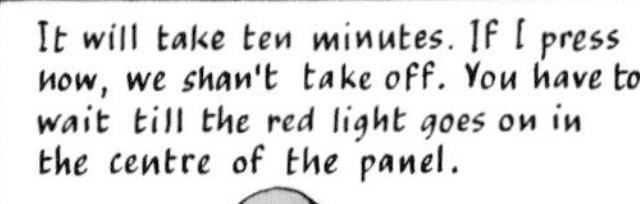
It will take ten minutes. If I press now, we shan't take off. You have to wait till the red light goes on in the centre of the panel.

Tank calling Moon-Rocket. We're nearly home. Let down the ladder and open the doors. Hello, Moon-Rocket...

I tell you, there's something fishy going on inside that thundering rocket!
Aren't you ready yet?

Nearly... only another three minutes.

Moon-Rocket, Moon-Rocket! What are you playing at? Answer me!

This is Tank calling Moon-Rocket... Tank calling Moon-Rocket... Can you hear me?
Stand by... Get ready... I'm going to press the button!

?
!
!

What the devil... The rocket !... Look... It's going...

No... it's fallen back... The engine has stop-ped !

?
?

Great sunspots! The rocket's off balance... It's sway-ing... It's going to fall on its side!

No, thank goodness! It's still upright! ... But what lunatic suddenly decided to set off the launch-ing mechanism?

Confound it! We're back on the ground. What's hap-pened, Wolff?

I... I don't understand. We began to rise normally... then the engine simply stopped. There's no reason at all...

Where's the prize nincompoop who pulled this half-witted stunt? Blistering barnacles, I've got a thing or two to say to him!...

Ah, it just occurs to me, Wolff... You and your conscientious scruples... If you've sabotaged the launching gear, I swear you'll pay dearly for it!

Me? Sabotaged it? How could I have done? W-what are you doing? ... NO!... NO!

Listen to me, Wolff. I'll count up to ten. If we're not safely on our way by the time I get to ten, I'll put a bullet through your brains!

Hello, Tintin... Wolff? Come on, why don't you answer? Thundering typhoons, open up!

Four... five... six...
Mercy! I beg of you! Mercy!

Seven... eight... nine...

And ten! The rocket's not moved. You asked for it, Wolff! I'll fire...

AAAAHH!

TINTIN!

Yes, me!... Did I disturb you? I do beg your pardon. I really should have knocked before I came in. Now get up, both of you, and put up your hands!

It's a small world, isn't it, Colonel Boris?... You haven't changed much since the days when you plotted against your master, the King of Syldavia.

By the way, you accused poor Wolff of having sabotaged the launching gear. I'm sorry to disillusion you: I was the culprit.

Tintin, Tintin, where are you?
Here, Captain. Come up quickly!

Billions of blue blistering barnacles! Where did this jack-pudding come from? Off the Moon?

No, out of the hold, where he was hiding — thanks to the treachery of our friend Wolff. Will you get busy tying them up, while we're waiting for the others?

Ah, there you are at last, Professor Calculus. Do come in. This gentleman is so anxious to make your acquaintance.

Who are you, sir? And what are you doing here?

So you prevented me from smoking my poor little pipe, Wolff, just to let this thundering Bashi-Bazouk have his ration of oxygen?

You may as well know at once that it's a waste of time questioning me. I'm not talking! You'd better interrogate Wolff: he'll be only too happy to spill the beans, the wood-louse!

In heaven's name, Wolff, what's the meaning of this? What's going on?... I can't make it out... It's all a misunderstanding, isn't it?... Come along, Wolff, tell me. Explain yourself.
I'm ashamed... So utterly ashamed...

Tintin!... Tintin!... Quick!
?

Quick, quick! I think Snowy's leg is broken!
What? I'm coming at once.

I'm afraid you're right. I saw him lying unconscious a few minutes ago. But there was other urgent work to be done. I'll carry him up to the cabin.

Well?
Yes, his leg's broken.

You hear that, you unfeeling monsters?... Vivisectionists!... Torturers!... Cannibals!

Anyway, who says that his leg's broken? Wait a minute; I'm going to have a look at it for myself.

Now then, Snowy boy. Captain Haddock's going to examine you... There... Let's see your paw... Does that hurt? No, not at all, eh?

!?
WOOAAAH

I...er...you see: I have a way with animals... It's one of my strong points. But I wonder if it wouldn't be better...

A few minutes later...
There we are, Snowy. A few days' rest, and you'll be fine.

Now then, back to these gentlemen. We're waiting for your explanation, Wolff.
Yes... I'll tell you everything.

Three years ago I was working in America at the rocket proving ground at White Sands. None of this would have occurred if I'd not had a passion for gambling... I got into debt... Then one day, in New York, a man approached me. He said he knew my situation, and was ready to settle my debts in exchange for a little harmless information.. ..

...about the nuclear research I was engaged on. But little by little he put pressure on me to reveal real secrets. At first, I refused. But my creditors were hounding me. I was trapped... Finally I gave in... A spy - that's what I had become. But one day I rebelled. I wanted to become an honest man again, and I fled to Europe... In the end I came to Syldavia, where I heard they were building an atomic centre. I got a job there.

When you arrived in Sprodj I was happy, and had forgotten the whole business. Then one day I received a message. They had picked up my trail; they ordered me to furnish them with complete details of the experimental rocket we were just finishing. Otherwise my past would be revealed. Heart-stricken, I surrendered.

So it was you who betrayed all the plans, and all the radio-control data!
It was I; yes, it was I.

Then it was you who nearly stove my head in, too, when I was lying in wait in the corridor at the Centre. Well, you'll pay for that all right!

One moment, Captain. We too have a question to ask the prisoner.
Yes, a vital question!

What about the skeleton, Wolff? Was that you?
Yes, skeleton, were you the Wolff? Come on, answer up!

Blistering barnacles, this is a SERIOUS interrogation! In other words, anacoluthons, you keep out of it!

All right, Wolff. Go on.

Well, thanks to Tintin, your enemies didn't succeed in capturing the trial rocket: you blew it up in flight. But they believed that it was I who betrayed them, and they threatened to kill me. Then they learned that this rocket was under construction, and they gave me fresh orders... One of the crates coming from Oberköchen would be faked, and would conceal a journalist. My part would be simply to facilitate his task...

And you believed a fairy-tale like that? You two-faced traitor! A cock-and-bull story! It would make a cat laugh!
Er... they said he'd reveal his presence once the rocket reached the Moon.

Then, soon after our arrival here, I took advantage of your absence to let him out of his hiding place. It was Jorgen. He divulged his real objective: to capture the rocket and take it back, not to Sprodj, but to the country for which he works.

Two more points, Wolff... The ladder being retracted... and the crate that nearly squashed us: was that you?
Yes!... And when you were just behind me pretending to have an attack of dizziness, you meant to push me out into space, eh, gangster?

And I trusted you implicitly... Oh! Wolff!...

Well, go on.
Yes, out with it, Judas!

Today, when Tintin was alone on board and the rest of you had departed for forty-eight hours, the Colonel decided to act. At the given moment, Tintin went down into the hold...
That's to say, you'd been first, to set your accomplice free. Then you managed to arrange that I'd go down myself.

Er... yes... I stayed here, and it was he who knocked out Tintin. It was only afterwards that he told me of his plan to abandon you on the Moon. I tried to stop him... I swear I did!

I believe you. This is what happened then... When I came round I was in the hold, trussed up like a chicken... I heard the humming of the motor, and realised what was going on... Luckily for us, these two worthy characters were never Boy Scouts!

I mean that they don't know how to tie a knot! So I managed to get rid of my ropes without too much difficulty. And none too soon! The engine was just starting. As the rocket was rising, I severed all the leads. The motor stopped immediately, and the rocket fell back to the ground...
And thanks to Tintin, we were saved!

Saved?... Ah, my poor friends, I only hope that you are not rejoicing too soon!

Undoubtedly by cutting the leads Tintin averted disaster... for the time being. Alas, it is only too likely that in falling, the rocket suffered serious damage. And this will probably take time to repair. Meanwhile, there's still the grave problem of the oxygen... But let's hear the rest of your story, Tintin.

Where was I ?... Oh yes. Once the rocket grounded, I opened the door of the air-lock and lowered the retractable ladder, so that you could get in. Then, having armed myself with a pistol and spanner, I came quietly up to the cabin... I found myself right in the middle of a family squabble...

This thug accused Wolff of sabotaging the launching gear, and was going to shoot him. My spanner knocked his gun out of his hand. Just in time, wasn't it, my dear Jorgen... as it seems that you are no longer Colonel Boris.
Why, do you know this pithecanthropus ?

Oh yes, we met in Syldavia, over that business of King Ottokar's Sceptre. Under the name of Boris, he was aide-de-camp to King Muskar XII, whom he shamefully betrayed. I won the first round, but for a while he seemed to be winning the second...

And now we'll dump these two down in the hold.

What ?... While we risk running out of oxygen, we're going to clutter the place up with these pirates ? They were going to abandon us on the Moon: well, that's the fate they deserve themselves, by thunder !

We must be more chivalrous than they were, Captain... Now, you're the expert, so take them below and tie them up securely.
As you like ! But you'll live to regret your noble gesture. Mark my words : you'll regret it !

Anyway, my little lambs, I'm going to knit you lovely little rope waistcoats to keep you nice and warm! Hand-made, by thunder! Guaranteed absolutely perfect !

Do what you like with me. But please be kind enough to stop spluttering in my face - it's wet !
!

What ?... Me ?... Wet ?... Blistering barnacles, you dare... A man of spirit like me ! To hear myself insulted, by this creature, this Bashi-bazouk !
Calm down, Captain, calm down !

Calm down ? Calm down ?... But you heard him, this little black-beetle ! Daring to make out that I'm wet ! Calm down ! I like that, from you !

To call me wet !... What a nerve !

Calculus has got one.
Yes, I'll fetch it.

!?

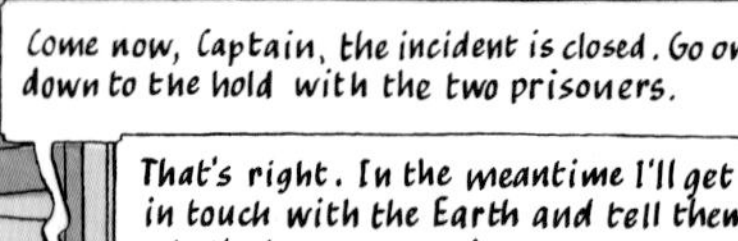
Come now, Captain, the incident is closed. Go on down to the hold with the two prisoners.
That's right. In the meantime I'll get in touch with the Earth and tell them what's been happening.

Moon-Rocket calling Earth. There have been extremely serious developments here... A traitor, in the service of some unknown Power, was secretely smuggled aboard the rocket.

... Wolff was his accomplice... Yes, Wolff!... Today they went into action and tried to seize control of the rocket. Fortunately we have managed to overpower them, and put a stop to their mischief...

Meanwhile...
There! If you succeed in getting yourselves undone, blistering barnacles, I'll sign the pledge and drink nothing but water for the rest of my days!

A few minutes later...
That's done! Our two chump chops are now on ice!
Good. Now for my news...

I've just made a superficial inspection of the damage to the rocket. My preliminary estimate is that it will take us at least a hundred hours to effect the necessary repairs.

To that must be added the time for our return journey. We have oxygen supplies for a hundred hours at the most, which means that having used our last resources to re-launch the rocket, we shall run the risk of arriving on Earth as corpses.

Perhaps! But meanwhile we're still very much alive. And we'll start work at once. At all costs we must get everything finished in the shortest possible time!

Moon-Rocket to Earth. We're going to begin the repair work. Give us some music: it will keep up our morale.

Earth to Moon-Rocket. We'll switch on Radio-Klow for you. Keep your spirits up!

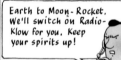

Come on, come on, cry-babies! To work! And none of those gloomy thoughts. We're going to have some music. Thundering typhoons, there's nothing like a bit of music to cheer you up!

This is Radio-Klow. Our programme continues with "The Gravedigger", by Schubert.

The time passes... Slowly, the lunar night falls on the desolate landscape...

wenty-two hours have gone by.

Moon-Rocket to Earth... The work is well ahead. Barring accidents, we shall have finished by midday... However, we are having to abandon the tank and the optical instruments on the Moon. To dismantle them and then reload them would take too long, in view of the little oxygen remaining.

We are only keeping the recording instruments, the cameras, and, of course, the oxygen cylinders from the tank. They constitute our final reserves. Tintin and the Captain have gone to collect them. I'm switching over now, as I want to keep in touch with them.

Right.

Hello Tintin... Calculus here... How are you getting on?

All right, thanks. But the sun has completely vanished. Only the mountain-tops are still glowing on the horizon...

But it's not preventing us from seeing, as there's a wonderful light from the Earth.
Pom Pom Pom ♩♪ And they danced ♪ by the ♩ light of ♩ the Earth

We have left a message sealed inside the tank for those who may one day follow in our steps. If we are lost with all hands, this message will be a reminder of the fantastic adventures of the first men on the Moon. Now we are coming back on board.

A few minutes later...

Everything's in order, Professor.

Good. Well, I've finished all the repairs. Earth have just given me the result of their reckoning. Take-off should be at 1652 hours. So we have about two hours to go.

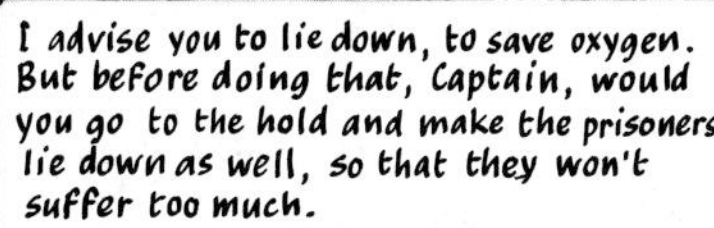

I advise you to lie down, to save oxygen. But before doing that, Captain, would you go to the hold and make the prisoners lie down as well, so that they won't suffer too much.

What?? And would you like me to take them breakfast in bed?

Keeping them is crazy enough! But to coddle them like babes in arms ... blistering barnacles, that's the limit! Still, I'll go.

Patience! I've not struck my last blow yet! But ssh! Someone's coming...

Two hours later...
Earth calling Moon-Rocket... Stand by ... Stand by...

Thirty seconds to go... Twenty seconds to go... Ten seconds to go... nine... eight... seven... six... five... four ... three... two... one... ZERO!

I press the button... and pray that everything works properly! Otherwise, we're condemned to death!

Success!... Wonderful!...
Marvellous!... We're off!

And just for a change, blistering barnacles, we're going to pass out!

And upon the shadowy world a few footsteps remain, the only trace of the first EXPLORERS ON THE MOON.

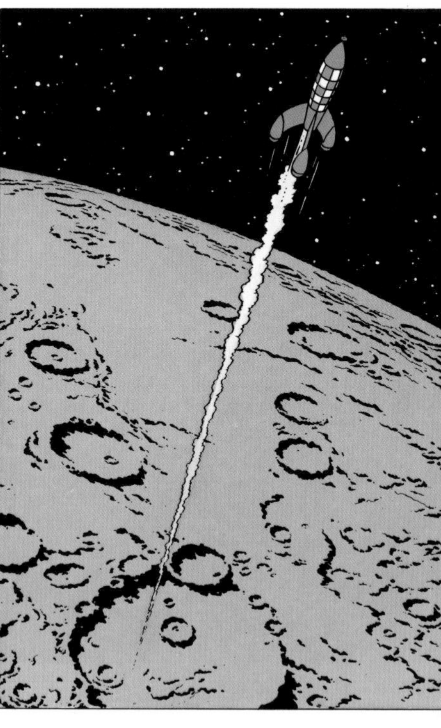

They're on their way! The only thing that matters now is that they should have enough oxygen... But whatever happens, everything must be prepared for landing.

Is that the landing site? Giovanni? ... Baxter here... If all goes well, the rocket will be here later today. Make sure everything's ready for their arrival; fire engines, ambulances... And get some electric saws ready, too, in case they haven't the strength to open the doors themselves. That's all for the moment.

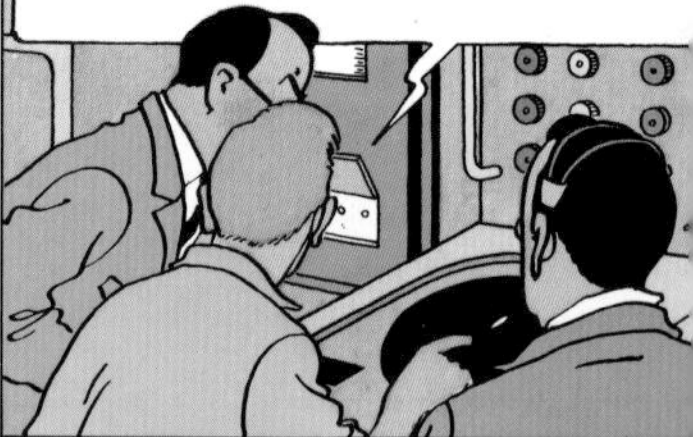
I say, Mr. Baxter, there's something wrong! Look: the rocket is deviating from the correct line of flight. I wonder what's happening...

By Jupiter! You're right! Perhaps the steering gear was damaged by the fall... Or else their gyroscopes have been put out of order... It's imperative that they correct their course... Call them, Walter!

This is Earth calling Moon-Rocket... Earth calling Moon-Rocket ... Are you receiving me?...

No reply!... And they're getting further and further away! The poor devils! They're going to their death!

Earth calling Moon-Rocket... Are you receiving me?

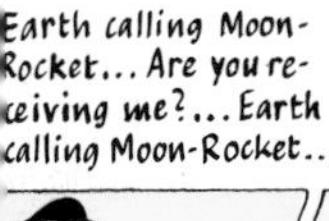
Earth calling Moon-Rocket... Are you receiving me?... Earth calling Moon-Rocket...

Earth calling Moon-Rocket...

Earth calling Moon-Rocket...

Oh, the poor devils! ... So much oxygen, simply being wasted ... Heaven knows, they have little enough to play with...
Ssh!...They're answering!

Moon-Rocket to Earth...This is Tintin calling...I have just regained consciousness.
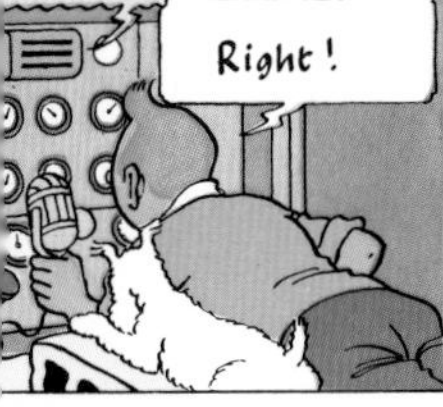
Earth to Moon-Rocket... Correct your line of flight at once: you are completely off course.
Right!

Quickly, Professor! Hurry! Come to the control cabin. We are off course!

I say! Where are you rushing off to like that?

Hi! Wait for me! I'm coming! What's happening?

Goodness gracious! This is disastrous! We're heading towards Jupiter!

Obviously the steering gear is out of alignment... Ah! That's done it, thank goodness!

Moon-Rocket to Earth...The steering gear was jammed... We are getting back on the right course.

Earth to Moon-Rocket...Well done! You're doing fine now!

Good. We can go below. That was a near thing!

And now that traitor Wolff isn't here to be such a kill-joy, we'll just cheer ourselves up. Let's have a drink all round... Tintin?... Professor?
By the way, where have the two detectives gone?

!
?
!
I'm just in time to bring you news of them!

Come on, hands up! ... That's right ... The boot's on the other foot now, isn't it, gentlemen ?! Congratulations: you have two brilliant colleagues behind those moustaches!

Ha! ha! ha! ... When they came to check on our ropes, they decided that handcuffs would be more secure! ... And I'm ready to bet they won't get them undone in a hurry

But that's enough talk! Gentlemen: you know the position. There isn't enough oxygen to go round. There are too many of us here. You spared my life: but I'm not going to spare yours!

But ... but ... you gave me your word that they would come to no harm.
And you were silly enough to believe me! ... Out of my way: let me finish them off!

No, Jorgen, no! ... You shall not do it! ... Never!
What's got into you? Let go of me!

Will you get out! ... Let go! ... Let go of that, you fool!
Hold him, Wolff!

BANG!
Earth to Moon-Rocket ... What's happened? We heard something that sounded like a shot ...

It's all over. Nothin
we can do.

Moon-Rocket to Earth ... Calculus here ... I ... It's terrible ... Jorgen managed to free himself ... He wanted to kill us ... and Wolff intervened ... There was a fight ... Jorgen had a gun in his hand ... and in the struggle it went off ... Jorgen was shot right through the heart.

I ... I didn't mean to ... He did it ... himself ...
I know, Wolff. You needn't blame yourself for what has just happened ... Here are your glasses ... Come and take your place among us again: I trust you.

What!! This interplanetary-pirate! This fresh-water-spaceman! Let him go free! Then, at the first opportunity this snake can ... can stab us in the back! Into the hold with him, blistering barnacles! Into the hold, and in irons!

But ... I ... What's ... what the matter with me?

I understand; carbon dioxide is accumulating...and when you work yourself up...
He's right, Captain. Do please keep calm!

You do as you like! But on your own head be it if we have trouble from this scorpion, Wolff! I disclaim all responsibility!

Don't worry, nothing will happen. I'll answer for him. Now, it will be better to lie on our bunks: in that way we'll save oxygen.

But first of all we must go and release the two detectives... And what shall we do about Jorgen's body?...
The only answer is to leave it in space.

A few minutes later...
Earth to Moon-Rocket... Here is your latest position... You are now 31,000 miles from your point of departure... How are things going on board?

Moon-Rocket to Earth... The carbon dioxide is getting worse and worse... It's hard to breathe now... but still, for the moment, things are bearable...

The others are dozing on their bunks. I'm having to struggle to keep myself from falling asleep.

Earth to Moon-Rocket ... Don't struggle, Tintin. Go to sleep. We'll wake you up when it's time for the turning operation.

Time goes by...
I think the coast is clear now. Everybody's asleep. This is my chance.

Let's hope no one wakes up! ... No, all's well.

Where are you going, Wolff?

Ssh! Not so loud!...I'm going below, to the hold to...er... I think there's another cylinder of oxygen down there.
Oh, good.

I had to ask, you see. The Captain particularly told me to give him details of every single move you made.

It's incredible... He hasn't given the alarm... Fate is on my side: I shall succeed!
Zzzz...
Zzzz...

Half an hour later...
Earth calling Moon-Rocket... Can you hear me?.. Earth calling Moon-Rocket... Can you hear me?...

Can you hear me?... MOON-ROCKET!
What?...What's that?... Oh yes, the radio...

Moon-Rocket to Earth...Tintin here...
Ah! You really scared us!

Stand by... You have a quarter of an hour to go before the turning operation.
Right. We'll get ready. I'll wake up the others.

Wake up!... Everybody on the alert! Put on your magnetic-soled boots. In a quarter of an hour we have to turn the rocket round.
!

Ugh! More of those confounded acrobatics! I was just dreaming that I was by my fireside at Marlinspike, with my cat on my knee...and instead...

WOLFF!... Blistering barnacles, where's Wolff?... His bunk's empty!

Don't worry, Captain, I know where Wolff is... He went down to the hold a few minutes ago.

And you let him go, you nitwitted ninepin, you?... Even when I'd told you to keep an eye on him?
I did keep an eye on him; he told me himself he was going to the hold.

And you were so keen to play the big-hearted hero!... Heaven knows what treachery that wolf in sheep's clothing is cooking up for us!...

Down to the hold, quick! It may not be too late!

What sitting ducks we'll make if our friend decides to have a little target-practice!

Now, where's he hiding, the gangster!

Thousands of thundering typhoons! There!... What did I tell you?... Look!

The brute!... The cannibal! He's sabotaged the... the things... er... the doings... I mean, the whatnots!
Look, a letter.

Great snakes! The poor, poor wretch!... This is horrible!
What? What is it? Read it out.

By the time you read this I shall have left the rocket...
When I am gone, I hope you will have enough oxygen to reach earth alive.
Perhaps by some miracle I shall escape too.
Forgive me for the harm I have done you —
Wolff

What! It can't be true! If he'd opened the outer door the motor would have stopped.
Wait, there's some more...

P.S.
To open the outer door without sounding the alarm and stopping the motors, I had to cut a few wires.
You only need to reconnect them, and everything will work properly again.
W.

Ten thousand thundering typhoons! He has gone out into space to save our lives!... And I accused him...

Yes, Captain. But even so, perhaps his sacrifice will be in vain... You go on up. I'll just repair these wires...

Ah, there you are. Well, have you caught that thug Wolff?
?

What? What did you say? Wolff a thug?! If ever I hear you say one disrespectful thing about that hero, I'll throw you into space to join him! You understand, you iconoclast, you?!

At that moment...
Earth to Moon-Rocket... Stand by... Ten minutes to go before the turning operation.
Right.

A quarter of an hour later...
Earth to Moon-Rocket... Turning operation successfully accomplished. Don't give in! In less than two hours you will be back on the Earth.

Yes!... And they'll give us an impressive memorial! I can see it from here! To Captain Haddock, a martyr in the cause of Science, etcetera, etcetera!

Well, if I have to die, then at least let it be in the way I choose, blistering barnacles!
Captain! What are you going to do?

What am I going to do? Thundering typhoons, I'm going to empty this bottle of whisky! Alcohol is a poison that kills slowly, they say... As slowly as it likes...

...so as far as I am concerned! It can take its time. I'm in no hurry!
That's enough, Captain! Go and lie down. This is no time to get drunk! ...

Blistering barnacles, why not? Was I or was I not told that the spirits on board were reserved for an emergency? Well, wasn't I?...

It's a thousand to one that we're going to end up as a crate of kippers! Ten thousand thundering typhoons, isn't that an emergency?!

Captain, I would remind you that drunkenness on the public highway is against the law. Go and lie down!

You... you two... ect-ectoplasms!... They needed two P-P-Punch- and Judy men on the p-pier... You-you sh-sh-should have stayed there...

This time we demand an apology!
Yes, we apologise on demand!

F-F-four to one... I... I give.... give up...

Half-an-hour later...
Moon-Rocket to Earth...The air's becoming unbreathable ... The last cylinder from the space-suits has been used up... The others are already unconscious... I wonder if we can possibly get back alive.

This is Baxter... Hang on, Tintin! You have only about fifty thousand miles to go... just about another hour. Courage, Tintin! Don't lose heart!... All will be well!

Thanks... Mr. Baxter... I'll do my best... to hold on till... the end... but I... I...

I'm afraid... I... shan't have... the strength... Goodbye!...Goodbye!

Goodbye! Yes, it's goodbye! May you all perish up there! Jorgen and Wolff bungled their work. We shall not get your accursed rocket... Well, may you go to the devil in it!...

For nearly an hour the rocket hurtles on towards the Earth.

Earth to Moon-Rocket... Stand by... You have only about 8,000 miles to go... Get ready to set the automatic pilot...

Moon-Rocket... to Earth... Tintin here... I understand... I... I'll try... to rouse... the... Professor.

Professor! Professor!... We're nearly home... Wake up... We've got to... set the automatic pilot...

Professor! For goodness' sake!... Professor please... It... it's no good... I can't rouse him... Now what's to be done?

I've... I've simply got to... try... myself... There's no one but me... Oh, I'm stifling...

I must... I must get to... to the ladder...

I've done it... But... shall I ever have the strength...

This... awful... dizziness!

Earth to Moon-Rocket... Are you in the control cabin?
Come on... one last effort...

Earth calling...
I'm nearly ...there...

Earth to Moon-Rocket... Earth to Moon-Rocket... Hurry up and set the automatic pilot... Earth to Moon-Rocket... Can you hear me?

Moon-Rocket... Can you hear me? ...Moon-Rocket!

Earth to Moon-Rocket... Can you hear me?... For heaven's sake answer!... There's not a moment to lose!... You are plunging to disaster!

Earth to Moon-Rocket! In heaven's name, Tintin, answer!

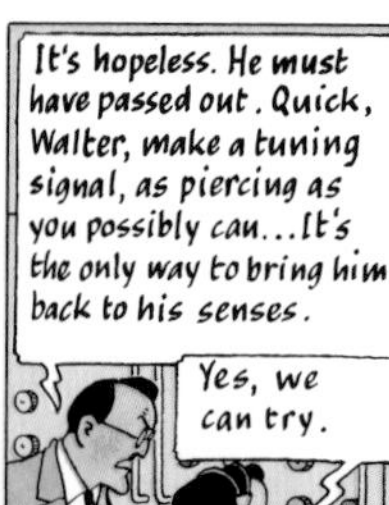
It's hopeless. He must have passed out. Quick, Walter, make a tuning signal, as piercing as you possibly can... It's the only way to bring him back to his senses.
Yes, we can try.

TRIIIUUUW

WOOUUIIIIII
TRIII
What?...Yes... yes ... I... the ...automatic pilot ...

WOOUIIIIIT

I...Hello...Tintin here... Stop...the whistling...I'm ...I'm just setting the automatic pilot...I...I... think that's done it...
Ah, just in time!

Well done, Tintin... Go and lie on your bunk now... Have you the strength to do that?...Hello Tintin?... Hello?

He must have fainted again... Never mind, he's done the essential thing... I'll dash over to the landing site now.

Right. We'll keep in touch with you by radio.

Observatory to Control... The rocket is only 900 miles from the Earth. In a few moments the auxiliary engine will take over from the nuclear motor.

... the rocket is now 550 miles away...

That's it...The nuclear motor has just cut out. The auxiliary engine will start up in a moment or two... But what's happening?

Great Scott!...The auxiliary engine hasn't started up...The rocket is hurtling towards the ground like a meteor!...They're going to be smashed to bits!

Hooray! The auxiliary engine has just started up at last!... In twenty minutes the rocket will touch down!
Let's pray they may still be alive!

Meanwhile at the landing site, observers anxiously search the sky for a sight of the rocket.

Look! There she is!

By Jupiter, look!... There's a car just setting off across the apron!

By thunder! It's Mr. Baxter's car! They obviously can't have seen the rocket coming! They'll risk it falling right on top of them... they'll be flattened ... or roasted!

Hurry up, driver... We must be well under cover before the rocket lands!

Help! The rocket! Stop, driver, stop!! ...

TSiiiii

Fire engines calling...The rocket has just landed... Mr. Baxter's car is hidden from us by a thick cloud of smoke!...

I'm afraid the car must be burning and its occupants... No! no!... There they are!

Ah, Mr. Baxter! What a terrible fright you gave us!... Not hurt?... No burns..?
No, nothing... But the rocket... Call the rocket!

Calling Moon-Rocket...You have landed!... Open the door... Moon-Rocket?... Moon - Rocket?

Moon-Rocket...The gantries are being moved into position... Moon-Rocket, I repeat, open the door!
No answer... We must cut open the hull... Bring the electric saws.

A few minutes later...
Hurry!... Hurry!

There, that's done it!

Now for the door of the air-lock! This one can be opened from the outside!

There... Heavens, not a sound! I feel as if I'm entering a tomb...

rofessor! ...Tintin!
.. Captain!...

Are we too late? Not a single move-ment! Hello! HELLO!

Professor!... Here, Professor!... Professor! ...It's no good.

Take them into the fresh air at once, and give them oxygen!... Hurry! ... I'll take care of Tin-tin: he must be up in the control cabin...

A few minutes later . . .
Success! He's opening his eyes...

I... where am I... What's happened? ... The rocket...
Don't worry now... You're safe and sound... back on Earth.
42138

Safe and sound... Back on Earth?... On Earth?... Is it really true... But the others?... And Snowy?
The Professor and the detec-tives are out of danger. So is Snowy... But...
But?...

Your friend the Captain ...alas, his condition is far more serious ... and I fear...
What are you trying to say?... Where is he?

He's over there... on that stretcher.
Good heavens!

The Captain!... It's not possible! ... Captain!

Captain!... Captain!... It's me, Tintin... Please, please wake up!... We're back home... Captain! Captain!

No sign of life... Do you really believe that...
Alas! His pulse is very irregu-lar, and very weak...

But what more can you expect?... The man's heart is worn out. But it's not surprising, if what they tell me is true. It seems that he was a great whisky drinker.

What?... That wasn't a dream!... I distinctly heard it. Someone here just mentioned whisky!!

Captain! My dear Captain!... Saved!... Heavens, what a fright you gave us!
A fright? You didn't really believe brave old Captain Haddock was going to let himself be snuffed out, did you? Now then, where is that whisky?
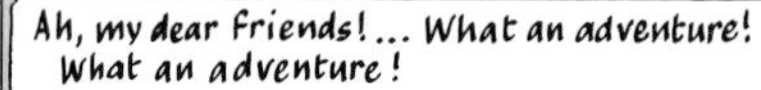

Ah, my dear friends!... What an adventure! What an adventure!
Here comes the conqueror of the Moon!

Cuthbert!... Let me shake your hand, old friend!
Well, Snowy! That's the narrowest escape we've ever had!

Here is the whisky you ordered, sir
Hooray!

A glass for me too, Captain. I want to drink a toast with you! It's the first time in my life I have tasted this beverage. But this is not the moment to drink camomile tea!
And how!

My friends, we have just lived through the greatest epic of all time: the marks of our feet are inscribed upon the surface of the Moon. And shall we let the dust of centuries hide those glorious marks for ever, gentlemen?

No, that will never be! For I promise you that we shall return there!
!

What? Us go back there? To the Moon? Me go back to the Moon?!

May I be turned into a bollard, blistering barnacles, if I so much as set foot in your flying coffin again! Never, d'you hear? You interplanetary goat, you! Never!!

I tell you, I've learned just one thing from all this: MAN'S PROPER PLACE...

?
42138

... IS ON DEAR OLD EARTH!

THE END